Also by Julie B Cosgrove

Relatively Seeking Mysteries

One Leaf Too Many
Fallen Leaf
Leaf Me Alone

Bunco Biddies Series

Dumpster Dicing
Baby Bunco
Threes, Sixes & Thieves
'Til Dice Do Us Part

WORD

HAS IT

by

JULIE B. COSGROVE

P

Write Integrity Press, LLC

Word Has It
© 2021 Julie B Cosgrove

ISBN: 978-1-944120-61-0

Scripture references are taken from The New International Version ®NIV ®. Copyright © 1973, 1978, 1984, 2011 by Biblica, Inc. ™ Used by permission of Zondervan. All rights reserved worldwide. www.zondervan.com.

 Published by Pursued:
an imprint of Write Integrity Press, LLC
PO Box 702852
Dallas, TX 75370

Find out more about the author, Julie B Cosgrove, at her website: www.juliebcosgrove.com
or on her author page at www.WriteIntegrity.com.

Printed in the United States of America.

DEDICATION

To Melissa, my niece, who understands
small town life. Thank you for supporting
my writing and for your prayers.

Contents

CAST OF CHARACTERS

Wanda Lee Warner – A widow who loves word games. She has lived in Scrub Oak, TX most of her life, and has a natural curiosity about events in her town because she loves her community and its residents. She has a dachshund named Sophie.

Betty Sue Simpson – Wanda's best friend since they were kids. She is also a widow. As a retired elementary school teacher, she knows the background of almost everyone who has lived in town since 1965. She also likes word games and puzzles.

Evelyn Joseph – Wanda's next door neighbor. She moved to Scrub Oak ten years ago to care for her sister until she passed from cancer. The widow of an Navy Intelligence officer who was killed in the Gulf War in 1990, she never remarried. She stayed in Scrub Oak because she and Wanda became good friends, and she wanted to finally put down roots.

Todd Martin – Wanda's nephew, who has returned to Scrub Oak to join the police force. They have always been close and enjoy a good game of Scrabble together on Thursday mornings before his shift. He lived with Wanda during his high school years after his parents divorced.

Hazel Perks – a neighbor who lives near the old, abandoned Ferguson Mansion and is an avid gardener. Gardening also keeps her aware of the goings on in her neighborhood. She grows prize roses.

Aurora Stewart – a "trophy wife" who lives across the lake from the Woodway Resort. She likes her privacy.

Mayor Arnold Porter – has been the mayor of Scrub Oak for over twenty years. He is rather pompous about his power but deep down has the community's best interests at heart.

Chief Brooks – the police chief of Scrub Oak. All business and a stickler for rules, but underneath he has a soft heart.

Pastor Bob Thomas – the clergyman at Holy Hill Church where Wanda attends.

Fred Ballinger – the retired principal of the Scrub Oak's lower school. He has eyes for Betty Sue.

Priscilla Tucker – owns the Coffee Bean, a local coffee shop that sells organic roasts from all over the world. Her sister, Sally, runs Sally's Salads which also features the organic blends.

Carl Smithers – owns the used car lot, gas station, and mechanic shop in town. He is a take-charge guy and has an overinflated view of himself.

Ray O'Malley – owner of the Hook & Owl Irish pub, which also makes great Irish stew, Evelyn's favorite.

Sally Ibson – owns Sally's Salads, but she also serves breakfast breads and coffee from her sister's Coffee Bean.

Barbara Mills – The librarian. She is also secretary for the City Council and local Audubon Society.

Pastor Paul Richardson – clergyman for First Baptist where Evelyn attends. Due to the COVID pandemic, he developed a large online following, does spots for the local Christian radio station, and has visions of going national.

Beverly Newby – owner of Anna's Antiques, named after her grandmother, who was an avid collector of Victorian pieces. Kathy King is her daughter.

Tom Jacobs – owner of Tom's Thrift Shop and local editor for the Oakmont County Weekly Gazette. His wife is Misty.

Kathy King – owner of Bargain Boutiques. Her husband, Jay is the insurance agent in town.

Schiller & Smith – the local attorneys Aurora Stewart used to try and sue Wanda. They also handle the Ferguson estate, which is still in probate.

Adam Arthur – the local fire chief.

Ben Bolton – owner of the Big B BBQ near the Woodway Resort. A gentle giant who used to play linebacker for the Dallas Cowboys back in the day. He also owns Better Burgers, but his sons run it.

Margaret Barrow – Wanda's sister who left Scrub Oak when Todd was in his early teens after she divorced her husband, Trent Martin, over having an affair with one of his college students in Fort Worth. Many in the town blamed her because she wanted to pursue a career in North Texas and traveled a lot.

Mr. Archibald Baker – an old man in the less affluent section of town who digs in trash cans for scraps to feed feral cats.

Ester Mae Fitzgerald – a new mother with a baby named Lucy, she is the organist at Holy Hill.

Zelda Lewis – runs Zelda's Zumba. She also teaches Pilates as well as other exercise and dance classes. She sells herbs and essential oils on the side. Her husband, Vlad, is a carpenter.

Collin and Claudia Rollins – runs A Cut Above, a barber/beauty salon that played only Christian contemporary songs. Collin manages the Grocery Mart.

Frank Patterson – a nice old guy with COPD from years of smoking foul-smelling stogies. He lives behind Wanda. Quiet, but his eyes see a lot that goes on. Now he sucks on thick pretzel sticks and always has one in his mouth.

Finn and Mary Lou Buckley – live across from Frank. She is the receptionist at Schiller and Smith. Finn, an extraordinary handyman, works odd jobs around town. Everyone calls him Fix-it Finn.

Melissa Suntych – an artist who lives on the edge of town off Woodway Drive and rescues animals, domestic and wild.

Scrub Oak Texas

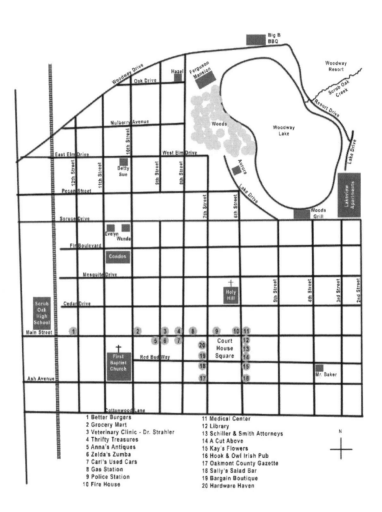

1 Better Burgers
2 Grocery Mart
3 Veterinary Clinic - Dr. Strahler
4 Thrifty Treasures
5 Anna's Antiques
6 Zelda's Zumba
7 Carl's Used Cars
8 Gas Station
9 Police Station
10 Fire House

11 Medical Center
12 Library
13 Schiller & Smith Attorneys
14 A Cut Above
15 Kay's Flowers
16 Hook & Owl Irish Pub
17 Oakmont County Gazette
18 Sally's Salad Bar
19 Bargain Boutique
20 Hardware Haven

CHAPTER ONE

"That is not a proper word, Todd."

Wanda Lee Warner huffed as she rose from the kitchen table to refill her glass of iced tea. She halted, swiveled back around, and reached down to flip her word tiles over in their little wooden stand.

"Really, Aunt Wanda." Todd Martin pushed his chair back. "I'm a cop. You think I'd cheat by peeking at your letters?"

She grunted in what she hoped sounded like a non-answer. "Want some more raspberry tea?"

"No, thanks." He came over to the counter and gave her a small side hug. "And 'perp' is a legitimate word." He showed her the dictionary entry on his cell phone screen.

She glanced at it and shrugged. "More banana nut bread?"

He snatched three slices from the plate and returned to the game they played every Thursday morning, his usual day off from patrol in Scrub Oak, Texas. Biting into one, he rolled his eyes. "Scrumptious."

"So, Monday marks six months since you graduated

from the academy in Austin. I am so glad you were hired on back here in our hometown." She took the remaining slices from his hand and placed them on a plate she'd set in front of him.

He nodded as he sat back down at the kitchen table. "I was afraid that what the Bible says is true."

"Oh?" She tried to keep her eyebrows from shooting into her widow's peak as she, too, returned to the game. For Wanda, the Bible was always true.

Todd must have sensed her concern. He smiled and reached to pat her hand. "About a prophet not being accepted in his own town. I'm no prophet, but I thought it might apply to my situation." He chuckled. "I wasn't exactly the model teenager."

"True, but your parents' divorcing and trying to drag everyone in Scrub Oak to take sides put you in an awkward position. Carrie Ann, too. I think it's why your sister accepted that scholarship to Louisiana State."

"She loves Baton Rouge. Grades seem to be good. She has decided on getting her Master's in Restaurant Management after she graduates next year. Plus, she and Reginald seem to be getting serious."

"I know." Wanda sighed the weight of another loss from her heart. First her sister, Margaret, had moved away, devastated that her friends didn't share her anger over her husband, Professor Trent Martin's, indiscretion with one of his graduate students in Fort Worth. Instead, they blamed her for driving his eyes to wander because she chose to pursue a pharmaceutical marketing career that required her to travel over most of North Texas. Poor adolescent Todd had been relegated to become the babysitter of his little ten-year-old sister. Now she lived eight hours away and rarely came home, even for holidays.

At least Todd had returned to the fold. Wanda relished these few hours each week with him. Even as a child, he had shared her love for words. Word searches, Scrabble, word wheels, and the daily jumble puzzles in the Dallas newspaper. He loved them all as much as she did. As a result, his vocabulary had far exceeded his peers in school.

The bond remained tight and secure, even if he did use a much more modern dictionary than the dog-eared Webster's from his high school days that he had gifted her when he left for the University of Texas. He'd inscribed inside, "We will always have words with each other." His sharp wit enhanced his easy-going, brown-eyed charm.

She ran her hand over the cover. "Okay, then. If you want use 'perp,' go ahead. I'm still eighty-five points ahead of you."

"Since when did we tally up points? What happened to 'I don't care about scoring. I simply like making words?'" He mimicked her slightly graveled, sixty-two-year-old voice with a wink.

She took a long sip of her tea. "I only said that because you kept losing."

He ignored her comment, but she noticed the sides of his mouth wiggle upwards, just for a split-second. In Todd language, the minute gesture spoke volumes. She swallowed back the urge to tell him how much she loved him, too.

"Your turn." His eyes shifted to her face.

"Ha. J-E-W-E-L-S." Wanda placed her tiles, playing off the "e" in perp. She hummed as she added up her score.

Todd groaned.

She dug in the bag for five more tiles, her fingers flicking through the little wood squares hoping that either by osmosis or providence they'd choose what she wanted. "Todd, do you find life boring here after living in Austin for five years?"

He shook his head with emphasis. "Not really. I enjoy wandering about town, saying hi to folks. Especially since now most of them seem to respect me."

"Well, you did solve the mystery of who was defacing the lawn decorations on East Elm Street and Oak Drive. And in your second month on duty, too."

A slight flush crawled over his nicely chiseled cheeks as he played off the second e, making the word escape. He had inherited his father's classic manly features. At least Thomas had given his son that, the snake.

Wanda cleared her throat, as if expelling the last thought before she felt the need to confess it when she went to bed tonight. She always lived by the rule that one sleeps better with a clear conscience.

"Well, I shouldn't really be telling you, but . . ." Todd stopped mid-sentence and chewed the side of his lip.

14

"But you will." Wanda wiggled in her chair as she placed a "W", an "O", another "O" and a "D" to make the word "woods" off his word "escape."

He took his sweet time, casting his attention between his letters and the Scrabble board, avoiding eye contact. He appeared to relish in baiting her curiosity, of which she had an abundance. Not that she ever gossiped. Heavens no. But she did take pride in knowing what was happening in her own town.

Wanda counted the tiles played to keep her patience.

He placed Y-I-N-G under the "L" in jewel, landing on a double word square. Then he wrote his score on the tally sheet.

As he reached in the tile bag, he glanced at her face. "Yes, ma'am I will. Speaking of jewels. Recall the burglary at that jewelry store in Burleson Monday night?"

"Yes, I heard about it. That store has been there forever. Edward got my engagement ring there. Let's see. That would be forty years ago." The thought zipped her briefly into the past. He'd been so dashing. She still wondered why the good Lord took him from her.

"Really? I didn't know that." He gave a small shrug. "Anyway, there may be, I repeat *may* be, evidence that the thieves are laying low in this area."

"In Scrub Oak?"

"Well, maybe not in town. But around here. I'm only telling you because I want you to take extra precautions until they are apprehended. *If* they are nearby, that is. The

15

three burglars escaped in an unmarked delivery van, later abandoned under the expressway overpass near Alvarado."

Her gasp sucked in all the air in the room. Not so much about the robbery details but because the words she and Todd had created so far perplexed her even more.

Perp, jewels, escape, woods, lying. And in her hand, the letters spelled mansion.

Could it be the old Ferguson house on Woodway, which had been lying empty, was no longer vacant? It had been boarded up for several years because the heirs were still in a fierce legal battle. A perfect hideout.

Wanda didn't want to say anything. Not yet. She eyed the clock on the stove—10:45. Maybe Evelyn or Betty Sue would know something. Evelyn wouldn't be home from her Bible study until after twelve-thirty, but Betty Sue's Pilates class ended in fifteen minutes.

"Oh, dear. I am getting absent-minded. I forgot I have an appointment at eleven. Can we pick up where we left off on Sunday afternoon?"

Todd flashed her a forehead-scrunched expression. "Um, sure. Okay. Say one o'clock?"

Lame excuse. He usually stayed until noon on Thursdays. But it was all she could think of that wasn't an outright lie. She did want to grab Betty Sue at the end of the class and go for an early lunch, so they could . . . chat.

They both rose from the table, and she walked him to the backdoor. "Come to the eleven o'clock service and I'll fix us lunch afterwards. Egg salad sandwiches with bacon crumbles and chopped celery. Your favorite."

He pecked her cheek with his lips. "Bribery. I could arrest you, you know?"

Give me time and I might have some other people for you to arrest. Then he would be the town hero. Secure his position on the force. Maybe he'd even finally snag Sarah, his high school heartthrob that worked as a veterinary tech for Doc Strahler. Settle down, have babies, make chief of police, and live here forever.

Wanda waved to her nephew as he disappeared through the garden gate.

Julie B Cosgrove

CHAPTER TWO

Wanda briskly walked the four blocks to Zelda's Zumba. When she got there, she spotted Betty Sue wiping her neck with a towel and chatting with two other women from their church. The thumping music still echoed in the background, probably mimicking the panting participants' increased heart rates.

She waved, and the motion caught Betty Sue's attention. Her robin-egg blue eyes widened as she recognized Wanda, but then her brow crinkled into a question mark expression.

Wanda weaved her way through the gaggle of ladies, some leaving and others coming in for the next class.

"Hey, what are you doing here?" Betty Sue wrapped the towel around her neck.

"Coming to see you. Thought you might want to go to Sally's Salads for an early lunch."

"Yum. But I am a bit grungy."

"Not so bad. Really." Wanda glanced at the t-shirt slightly sticking to Betty Sue's diminishing frame. Her best friend had shed close to thirty pounds in the past six months. Wanda suddenly felt her own ripples of flab begging to poof out from her zippered slacks. Maybe she should join one of these classes. She followed Betty Sue to the foyer but stopped to grab a trifold brochure on the way out.

"They have a beginners' Pilates on Mondays and Fridays at nine in the morning. She starts you off slow and easy, so you won't waddle in pain the rest of the week."

Wanda blushed and slipped the schedule in her purse. Betty Sue obviously had not lost the eyes-in-the-back-of-her-head teacher feature even though she'd retired five years ago. That was when the pounds had piled on from couch-sitting and snacking while watching TV or reading. A widow's common plight to keep the lonely moods at bay. Wanda knew it all too well. Ten years into her widowhood life, she still fought the urge.

"And for what reason do I owe this pleasure?" Betty Sue swerved to miss a crack in the sidewalk protruding up from the pressure of an ancient live oak's roots. A squirrel in its bough reprimanded them for having the audacity to walk by.

"Todd told me something." She caught her friend's footsteps slowing as she swiveled to face Wanda. "Oh, nothing bad . . . Well, maybe. Not sure yet. Let's wait until we're seated. Then I'll explain."

Betty Sue cocked her head a bit to the right but complied. They walked the next block in silence.

When they arrived at the café, Wanda opened the door,

and immediately a blast of luscious cool air hit her face. After all that walking in the mid-eighty-degree weather, it felt good.

Betty Sue followed her inside and waved at Sally, who looked up from behind the clear plastic nose guard as she added more carrots and cucumbers to the myriad of bowls sitting in crushed ice.

"Hi, Ladies. I just set out the veggie selections. Come make your own salads."

Sally offered three plate sizes, each priced accordingly. Her patrons could pile on what they wanted from the varieties of choices from organic greens to pasta and chicken salads, even egg salad though Wanda avoided it. It couldn't beat her recipe with a stick. Muffins, crackers, and hot French bread slices lay at the next buffet section along with three cauldrons of piping hot soups. Bowls and bread plates were stacked like shiny white and blue striped soldiers at attention.

The ladies remained quiet as they made their selections, then decided to sit at one of the blue gingham-covered bistro tables near the wall. As Wanda reached for the pepper, Betty Sue leaned in. "Well?"

"Shouldn't we pray first?"

A slight sigh exited through her nose. "Of course. Sorry." Betty Sue bowed her head and offered a simple, three sentence thanks for their food, their salvation, and their friends.

"Amen." Wanda spread her navy cloth napkin in her

lap. "Okay, I will start at the beginning. Todd came over to play Scrabble, like he always does on Thursdays at nine."

Betty Sue stabbed a piece of arugula dripping with low-cal ranch with her fork and nodded as she lifted it to her mouth.

"Well, he happened to tell me that there might be a gang of robbers hanging out in this area. You know, from that burglary in Burleson?"

Betty Sue bobbed her head several times as she wiped her mouth. Her blue irises sparkled with interest and perhaps a tad bit of apprehension.

"He told me because he wants me to be extra aware of strangers. I figured you should know as well."

"Thanks."

"There is more. I think. Maybe not. I don't know." She ran her hand down her water glass and flicked off a few drops of condensation.

"Wanda Lee Warner, I have rarely seen you flustered. What is going on?" Betty Sue reached for her friend's hand. "Are you on steroids for your arthritis again? You know they make you antsy."

Wanda squeezed her friend's fingers and withdrew her hand. "No. But have you ever had the sensation that, as my grandmother used to say, someone tiptoed over your grave?"

"You mean a premonition?"

"Sort of. Here me out, then tell me if I need the pencils in my box sharpened." She tapped her temple and then proceeded to relay the words on the Scrabble board and what they made her think about.

After she finished, she sat back and watched Betty Sue's reaction. As a teacher, she'd seen everything and heard even more. She'd always had an analytical mind and besides being an avid reader, Betty Sue could complete the New York Times daily crossword puzzle within fifteen minutes, most days. "Well?"

"I am not sure, Wanda. I mean it could be a serendipity, or nothing at all. What other words were on that board?"

Wanda thought for a long moment. "I can't totally recall, but the board is still set up on my kitchen table. Want to come see?" Betty Sue lived two blocks north of her on 10th and Elm.

"Sure. It'll keep me from giving in and ordering Sally's hot gingerbread with lemon sauce."

"By the way. I walked. I didn't bring the car."

Betty Sue faked a shocked expression, then chuckled. "Good for you. I told you exercise would up your energy level. I always walk to Zumba and back."

They gobbled down the rest of their salads, paid, and power-walked back to Wanda's house on Spruce. By the time they got there, Wanda's knees were as wobbly as a dish of Jell-o on top of a washing machine in spin cycle. Her neck and back were sticky and her lungs complained about the abuse.

Wanda led Betty Sue down the driveway and through the gate to her kitchen door stoop. Very few people ever used the front doors in Scrub Oak unless they were selling something or delivering a package. They entered the kitchen and Wanda made a sweeping gesture toward the kitchen table as if she played a hostess on a TV game show. "I'm going to get a wet washcloth. Want one?"

"I'm fine. Thanks though." Betty Sue nodded then sat down where Todd had and studied the board. She called out to Wanda down the hall so she'd hear her over the running water in the bathroom. "I also see zero, reduce, candy, under, and panel."

"Yes, but . . ." Wanda returned and tapped the Scrabble board with her finger. "These words were spelled last. Right before and while we were talking about the burglary." She sat across from her friend. "I think Todd played 'perp' because he is a cop, and it is probably the first thing he thought of. In fact, I wasn't sure it was a word."

"Yes, that makes sense. So does the word 'escape' if that was on his mind. If you were talking about the case, then wouldn't it seem plausible that you both played words relating to it that floated to the forefront of your minds?"

"I played the word "jewel" before he even told me."

"Yes, but it has been in the *Gazette* and everyone is talking about it."

"Lying? Woods? Neither have anything to do with a burglary." She spun her rack to Betsy Sue's line of focus. "And check out the letter tiles in my hand. What word pops into your brain?"

"Mansion." It came out in almost a whisper. She

blinked and raised her attention to Wanda's face. "You think they are staked out at the old Ferguson house on Woodway, don't you?"

"It has been 'lying' vacant." She air-quoted the word. "Or is it laying?"

"Lying, I am fairly certain." Betty Sue's face took on the teacher-look.

"Whatever. But it does back up to the woods. Which Blake Ferguson, the original patriarch, purchased in 1919, if I recall correctly, so none of it would ever be developed." Wanda leaned back into the chair spindles and crossed her arms. "So?"

Betty Sue stood and tucked a brown curl behind her ear. "I don't know. Maybe you need to tell Todd."

"And have him believe that I am ready for assisted living? I don't think so." She huffed and went to the fridge. "Want some raspberry tea?"

Patting her tummy, which had flattened considerably in the past few months, her friend declined.

Wanda sucked her abs in a bit and leaned her backside against the counter.

"Woohoo. You two plotting the next coup without me?" Evelyn's shrill but melodious voice bounced off the moss-green siding outside before she clomped onto the deck and opened the kitchen door. Evelyn lived next door.

"Come in. Come in. We might be, but not exactly a coup. More like a conundrum."

"Or a crime?" Betty Sue wiggled her eyebrows. "If the

words define it correctly."

"What words? Don't tell me you two have been playing with a Ouija board. Pastor Jim at First Baptist tells us to steer clear of stuff like that." Evelyn harrumphed.

Wanda plastered on a *Who, me?* innocent face.

Evelyn waggled her finger. "Don't give me that look, Wanda Lee Warner. I've known you for almost ten years now. What are you up to? You always stick your nose where it doesn't belong."

"I do not."

Betty Sue grimaced and turned to Wanda. "Well, recall the time you thought Mr. Blake was rooting though people's trash to find out their personal info. Turns out he didn't have enough money to feed his four cats and was too embarrassed to say anything."

"Or the time you talked us into sitting by the lake all night because you swore you saw a flashlight shine across it?" Evelyn added. "You were sure a ring of thieves were casing the guests at the Woodway Resort last fall. It ended up being a reflection from Aurora Stewart's metal wind chimes hitting her new spotlights from her backyard across the way."

Wanda lifted a shoulder to her ear.

With both of her friends eyeing her as if *she* had robbed that jewelry store in Burleson, Wanda felt a chill sweep across her shoulder blades. What *was* she up to?

And why did it seem she always was the one to get into scrapes?

CHAPTER THREE

"Here's what I think. We do nothing. It is merely a coincidence." Evelyn reached under the sink for the plastic wrap. "But in case this does turn out to be of importance, I say we preserve the Scrabble board. As evidence."

Her late husband had been in Navy Intelligence under Bush-Senior. Evelyn watched every NCIS and CSI show on TV. She recorded them by date, crime, and city. Wanda guessed it somehow made her feel closer to his former line of work. Widows often had weird idiosyncrasies that few people, except other widows, understood.

"What good will that do? Can't we just take a picture. I mean, they don't need fingerprints or anything, right?" Betty Sue spread her palm and hovered it over the word tiles to stop Evelyn from mummifying the game in Saranwrap.

"She's right, Evelyn. A picture will suffice." Wanda took the roll from her friend and put it back in the slot in the wire rack. "Besides, Todd and I are scheduled to finish the game Sunday afternoon."

After taking pictures with her cell phone of the board

and the tiles in her rack, Wanda placed a tea towel over the letters and slid the board on top of the fridge. Then she put the racks inside the box and set it on top. "I am being silly. Evelyn is right. Only a mere coincidence."

But a wad of doubt sat in her gut the rest of the afternoon. As she dust-mopped the floor, tidied the counters even though they didn't need it, and rearranged the cooking utensils in the drawer, her eyes kept lifting to the top of the refrigerator. She felt like a kid with the cookie jar stuffed with snickerdoodles barely out of reach.

"Ugh. Enough." She stomped out of the kitchen, plopped in her easy chair, and opened the historical novel she had been reading until her eyelids drooped the night before. As if on cue, her black dachshund, Sophie, lumbered over and laid her chin on Wanda's right foot.

The next thing she knew, the duchess had been exonerated and the duke's nephew hauled off to the Tower of London. The end. The mantle clock chimed seven as she closed the book.

She added it to the basket for the library's used book bazaar next week and waddled back into the kitchen to heat up some leftovers.

The box on top of the fridge almost whispered her name as she sat at the kitchen table. She pushed her cheesy chicken and rice casserole around on the plate, took six bites and decided her stomach had handled enough. Besides, the recipe served six to eight, so she'd heated it up twice this week already. Maybe she'd freeze the rest and give it to

28

Todd on Sunday.

Gingerly, she reached up on tiptoes and took everything back down from on top of the refrigerator, uncovered the towel, and scooted the slightly misaligned tiles back into their places on the board with her pinkie finger.

Jewels. Woods. Perp. Lying. What did it mean?

Then there was the word mansion sitting in her tile rack. Well, it wouldn't hurt to stroll by the Ferguson place after dinner, would it? It was still light until almost eight o'clock now. She wouldn't venture inside the wrought iron fence onto the lawn—everyone in town knew that was a major no-no—just circle the block it sat on. Maybe she'd see a neighbor out watering their lawn in the cool of the evening. Catch a few fireflies emerging from the blades of the carpet grass in Pecan Park. Listen for that old hoot owl in the hollow of the sprawling tree at the corner of 9th and Oak.

Her hips and tummy would thank her for the exercise. Sophie would enjoy it as well. Decided.

Her whistle perked Sophie's floppy ears. When she saw the turquoise leash dangling from her master's fingers, she came plodding to her feet. Wanda hooked it to her collar and they headed out.

A fine evening, even though it still hovered in the high seventies and the humidity off the lake made the air seem a bit heavy. The blue sky had begun to dim, and off to the horizon, white cirrus clouds took on pink and orange hues near the far northern edge of the Texas Hill Country.

The pair strolled past the park and turned up 8th Street. Three elementary-aged kids whisked by on their bikes, giggling. She knew their names but only waved in silence. They lifted their chins in unison and sped around the corner.

Then, providence smiled on her. Hazel Peters watered her prize rose bushes along her front walk. They had never been the best of friends, but they remained acquaintances, often attending the same service at Holy Hill Church and sitting on the city beautification committee.

"Hi, Hazel."

The older woman jumped, then waved with the hose, almost drenching Sophie. "Oh, sorry."

Wanda walked up the sidewalk. "Your roses are really coming out now. Such gorgeous colors, especially the yellow ones with the blushed edges."

Hazel's cheeks took on the same color as the roses. "Thank you. I mix my own fertilizer, you know."

No, she didn't. And the idea made the casserole flip a bit in her tummy. "Good for you." Now, how to steer the conversation. "Any word on who will get the Ferguson house?"

She shook her head. "Haven't heard a peep in months. Though yesterday about this time, I did see two workmen go around the back. Not sure if they went inside or not. Never saw a light come on. Think they were contractors of some sort. Jeans and t-shirt types." She sniffed a slight disapproval.

"I see. Are there often people over there? I mean the lawn always looks nice."

"Oh, yes. Pete's Lawn Service comes every Tuesday morning from eight to ten, like clockwork."

Hmmm. Could it be the so-called contractors she saw on Wednesday were not that at all? The robbery was on Monday night according to Todd. If they waited until after the landscapers had left Tuesday morning, then they'd have a safe hideout for at least a week.

"Well, it is good to know it's being taken care of. Blake Ferguson, Jr. was so particular about his castle and the grounds, especially that maze."

Hazel agreed. "What surprises me is that no one patrols by there on a regular basis. I mean I know Scrub Oak is a small town with hardly any real crime, but that place must be chock-full of antiques, silver, and paintings. Who knows what all?"

Wanda hadn't considered that. "Well, have a good evening. I better get little Sophie home before dark."

"Good night." Hazel returned her attention to her roses.

Wanda glanced back down the lane at the mansion looming in the dusk like a sleepy giant assigned to overlook the town in case dragons descended. She chuckled to herself. Too many epic medieval novels. But Katy Huth Jones wrote them so very well. She'd read just about every one of them in her Mercy series.

Even so, Wanda couldn't ignore the eerie feeling she had about the abandoned chateau with its turrets, stately balconies, and peaked roofs. A shame, really. Someone should turn it into a museum, or a B&B, or something.

Then movement caught her eye. A figure dashing around the corner of the mansion, or only the sprawling oak branches playing tricks with their shadows in the sunset? She couldn't be sure.

But one thing she did know. The house needed watching. Especially if it still held valuables inside. If the police didn't have time, she and a few of her friends certainly did.

CHAPTER FOUR

That night Wanda sat in bed, her laptop propped up on her knees. She made up a schedule of two hour shifts over the next week. Perhaps she could get people to sign up for them. Those at night should probably be men, or neighbors who lived close enough on West Elm or 8th to have a view of the mansion from their upstairs windows.

Hazel might sign up and encourage the others on her block to do the same. Wanda figured it would benefit them to know a house lying vacant in their area was secure, right? In fact, wasn't it the town's duty to watch out for each other's properties?

Of course, it was. Wait, would she need the mayor's permission to set up a . . . what did they call it? Oh, yes. A neighborhood watch. Many cities had them, so why not Scrub Oak?

Yes, that way she could make sure the Ferguson House was properly guarded, and also secure the whole town. Burglars in the area, if they were there, could pilfer anyone's domains, rob the grocery, or even hit the stores like Hardware Haven or Anna's Antiques.

If she did need permission, she'd have to stand up before the entire town council—Mayor Arnold Porter, Pastor Paul Richardson of First Baptist, Carl Smithers who owned a full-service gas station and used car lot in town, retired principal Fred Ballinger, and the librarian, Barbara Mills, who served as secretary—this upcoming Monday and make her request.

Wanda threw back the covers and reset her alarm for seven o'clock. She had to be at the courthouse, where the city offices were, bright and early tomorrow to begin the process of petition. Then she hitched her breath. What to wear?

Her normal "uniform" of jeans or casual slacks with a knit blouse wouldn't do. She flicked through the hangers in her closet and chose her best spring outfit, the one she planned to wear on Easter Sunday. A linen dove gray skirt and jacket with a rose silk shell blouse. She'd wear her mother's pink pearl necklace with matching earrings. The combination accented the silver streaks in her dark brown hair that would be wrapped into a stately bun instead of her usual ponytail or French braid. Unlike a few women she knew, Wanda was proud of every gray strand. She had earned them, they commanded respect, and they gave her locks a softened, frosted appearance.

Pleased with her decisions, Wanda crawled under the covers, careful not to disturb her furry foot warmer who softly snored on the turned-back comforter at the foot of the bed.

W₄

A happy cardinal chirping for a mate woke Wanda ten minutes before the alarm tune on her cell phone sounded. She grunted and crawled out of bed. Sophie perked up, hopped off, and padded down the hall to the kitchen and her bowl.

"Yes, yes. I'm coming." Wanda pulled on her robe, shoved her cell phone in the pocket, and followed the wagging tail like an obedient servant. As the coffee perked, she let Sophie outside to do her thing. She poured the kibbles in the dog's bowl before dumping dry cereal into hers. Wanda examined the breakfast box, recalling the morning a few months ago when Sophie lapped up her food with extra vigor. Wanda had experienced a toss-and-turn night and felt extra drowsy that morning. It wasn't until she took her first spoonful that she realized her bowl contained the kibbles and Sophie's the Honey Nut Cheerios. She would never make that blunder again.

Almost an hour later, she climbed the steps and entered the large granite building that commanded the central position in their town and even throughout the county. Thankfully, at this early hour, there had been plenty of open parking spaces in the courthouse square. She could have walked the distance, but the humidity had risen and she hadn't wanted to perspire. As it was, even the short walk from her car beaded her forehead. The air conditioning that blasted her skin once she entered felt downright invigorating.

Her heel clicks echoed on the marbled tiles of the hallway leading to the Mayor's office. She tapped on the door, and his secretary, Lucia, beckoned her to come in.

"Good morning, Lucia. I wanted to know the procedure for something." She motioned to the chair catty-corner to the mahogany computer desk and received a nod.

"Thank you." She scooted the chair closer and retrieved her sign-up sheet from her satchel. "I think we all expected the Ferguson estate to be settled by now, but it seems the heirs are still locked in a battle. And as I walked my dog, Sophie, by it last evening, I stopped to speak with Hazel Peters. She was watering her roses. You know how often she has won prizes for them? Of course, you do. You are one of the judges of the garden club's lawn of the year awards every year."

"Hmm. Yes." Lucia shifted in her secretary chair. "You said something about a procedure?"

"Oh, of course. For organizing a neighborhood watch. I haven't been inside the Ferguson home since I was in lower school. Anita Ferguson, God rest her soul, used to have a formal tea for the eighth grade girls every May. But that was before your time."

"Yes, I suppose it was. Mrs. Warner . . ."

"Oh, call me Wanda, please. Anyway, I recall all these wonderful antiques, paintings, silver service sets, candelabras . . . you know. If they are still inside, well, and if word got around outside of this community that they were ripe for the pickings . . ."

"I see your point." The phone buzzed. "Excuse me." Lucia cradled the headset next to her shoulder. "Yes, sir?"

Wanda silently harrumphed. The poor girl would get a crick. Surely, she should have a Bluetooth. This was two decades into the twenty-first century, not the 1980's. Another issue to bring to the city council's attention, or at least the mayor's.

"Yes, sir." She hung up. "Mayor Porter says to come into his office. He overheard what you said and will speak with you concerning it."

"Oh, okay." Then she realized the door to his office had been partially open.

"This way." Lucia flashed her professional smile. Wanda wondered if she practiced it in the mirror.

The ladies rose from their chairs in unison. Wanda rubbed her palm down her skirt to make sure it was warm and dry when she shook the mayor's hand then stepped into his office. Even in a small town, the domain of the mayor's inner quarters, so to speak, oozed the demand for respect.

She and her parents had moved to the town in 1966 when she was eight. In all that time residing in Scrub Oak, she'd never set foot in here before. The police station several times, but that was a different matter entirely.

Her heels sunk into the lush maroon carpet, making her wobble for a second. *Good going, Miss Grace.* The office was decorated in dark mahogany furnishings, including a large executive desk, a credenza, and a row of bookshelves. Forrest green leather chairs perched in front of the desk and a green, burgundy, and tan patterned sofa sat against the other wall underneath a painting of the north Texas prairies and hills. A buckskin-colored winged chair angled next to it. Flanking the desk, an American flag and Texas state flag hung on brass standing poles like soldiers at attention. Framed awards and the current governor's picture formed a decoupage behind the desk.

Mayor Porter rose and extended his hand. "Mrs. Warner, please have a seat."

She firmed her grip in the handshake to show her strength and confidence, and then chose the chair on the right.

He returned to his executive perch and leaned back, fingers tented under his chin. "Did I hear correctly? You are concerned about the valuables in the Ferguson House?"

"Yes. And I thought it might behoove the residents of this fine community to form a neighborhood watch. Not just out of neighborly concern . . ." Had she said neighbor too much? ". . . but for our protection as well. I mean, just because we've not had any major crime in Scrub Oak since the 1950's when those train robbers jumped the tracks. And of course, there was the time the Woodlake Resort's safe was robbed. But that was an inside job, wasn't it?" She stopped to take a breath.

He gave her a fatherly, authoritative grin.

"Oh, I apologize. I sound like an old ninny rattling on so much. I don't know why I am so nervous. I've never been in here before." She pressed her hand to her pearls and gazed around the room. He must think her a nutcase.

"Mrs. Warner." He leaned forward and rested his hands on the desk blotter. "There is some merit in your idea. Unlike the one you had about Mr. Robert's trash can digging."

"Well, yes, that was an unfortunate misjudgment, I agree. But . . ."

"Or the flashlights shining on the resort that ended up being reflections of a windchime?"

Wanda raised her finger. "In all fairness, it was robbed three weeks earlier, as I said."

"True, but we both acknowledge it was an inside job. The young man who was convicted knew the layout quite well, and it was a full moon so no further illumination was necessary."

She bowed her head in agreement.

He cleared his throat. "However, this time your observations are worth considering. In fact, I have contacted the estate attorney several times about hiring a security guard but the heirs are unable to agree on the expense. The house does have a state of the art alarm system though. It was installed less than a year ago."

Wanda's ears perked. "After the Woodway Resort incident?"

"Uh, hmm. Yes." He rose from his chair. "Let me look

into this matter and discuss it with Chief Brooks. Perhaps it is time we had a neighborhood watch system in this town. Better to be pro-active."

Wanda smiled and shook his extended hand. "Thank you."

He led her to the outer office. "I am sure there are established protocols. I promise you, I will investigate it before the council meets Monday evening. I will have Lucia call you and set up an appointment time that morning if we need to discuss this further."

Wanda thanked him again. She felt proud as she strutted down the hallway back out into the Texas sunshine. Then, she halted on the courthouse steps as she reached in her purse for her sunglasses. He had been awfully accommodating.

She smacked her forehead. Of course. He was up for re-election in three weeks. And Chief Brooks would want to be reappointed the next term.

Wanda huffed. She needed a cinnamon roll. Heck with her tummy flab.

She strutted the three blocks to the Grocery Mart, her steaming angst competing with the Texas sun now beating on her back. Once inside she made a beeline to the Coffee Bean, run by her friend Priscilla Tucker. She greeted Wanda with a wave, then frowned.

"What's wrong?"

Wanda ordered and then told her.

"Well, he didn't say it was a bad idea." Priscilla Tucker

set the gooey treat in front of Wanda along with a vanilla latte. "And I agree. In fact, it is long overdue. Ever since Texas Monthly featured Woodway Lake as the best little-known getaway in the state last summer, we've had an increase in visitors. Who knows where they come from or who they are? Count me in."

"Into what?" A different voice echoed from behind them.

Wanda turned and saw Evelyn standing there.

"Hi, Wanda." She smiled and then addressed Priscilla. "I'll have a decaf mocha to go. I have a hair appointment in fifteen minutes."

"Plenty of time to chat. Want to sit?" Wanda grabbed her second breakfast and headed to one of the pink wrought iron table sets for two with brown and pink striped chair covers.

Evelyn joined her and eyed her cinnamon roll.

"Don't tell Betty Sue."

Priscilla set Evelyn's hot drink down, chuckled, and walked back to the register.

Evelyn took a sip. "Why would I? She's not your mother. Neither am I."

"I know, but since losing all that weight, she keeps hinting that I could get in better shape."

Her neighbor scoffed. "Who couldn't? So, I confess. I really came in because I saw you in your Easter best. What's up?"

"A meeting with the mayor."

"Oh, is that so?" One eyebrow arched.

Wanda gave her the shortened version of the events leading up to and including this morning's conversation. And her realization of its opportune timing.

"When my husband was alive, we joined a neighborhood watch in our Houston suburb. It's a national organization and usually a spokesman comes to speak and helps the watch get going. Ours was a Houston police officer. You don't need the mayor's permission. He should know that."

"Really?"

She swallowed the rest of her mocha. "I guess it was good of you to inform him of your interest, but frankly, if you want to start one, you can. All you have to do is hold a meeting. It would be nice to coordinate it with the police, though. Out of courtesy."

"Of course. I intend to do just that." Especially since Evelyn mentioned it. Getting on the wrong side of Chief Brooks would not be a great idea. The last thing Wanda wanted to do was soil Todd's reputation due to her inconsiderate behavior.

Evelyn rose and looked at the clock in the shape of a coffee pot. "Gotta run. Keep me posted."

Wanda turned to Priscilla who had been busy wiping the tables and most likely listening. "Well, could we have the meeting here?"

A huge grin filled her face. "Absolutely. And I will provide free drinks."

Wanda wiped off her hands and wadded up her napkin. Then she extended her right hand in a shake. "Deal. Tomorrow morning at ten?"

"Will that be enough time to get the word out?"

Wanda cocked her head. "Priscilla. This is Scrub Oak. Everyone will know by sunset."

"True."

"Know what?" Hazel wandered in with a vase of pink tea roses to decorate the counter.

Wanda and Priscilla laughed.

Julie B Cosgrove

CHAPTER FIVE

Hazel and Wanda walked down the block to the library to use the computers so they could design fliers. It was quicker than driving back to Wanda's house and there was no parking limit around the courthouse.

Barbara Mills had been the town's librarian as long as Wanda knew. Now an octogenarian, the lady still had a sharp mind and probably had read every book in the place. At least she knew enough about each one to recommend them.

"I will be happy to help. Here is the Wi-Fi password. And I tell you what. The library will donate up to fifty copies of the fliers. You just leave a small stack here and I will distribute them as people check out."

"Great. Thank you." Wanda and Hazel sat down and spent the next hour reading about neighborhood watches and signing up for the national newsletter as well as conducting an online chat with one of the North Texas organizers. They spent another half hour designing the flier until they were both satisfied it would attract attention and give enough, but not too much, information.

"I am going to text Betty Sue to bring tape and help us post them." Wanda patted Hazel's arm. "She's a retired schoolteacher, you know. They always have supplies like that lying around."

Ten minutes later, Betty Sue waltzed in with three dispensers and a smile. Her cheeks were as rosy as Hazel's bushes. "I jogged all the way."

"Shhhh." A man peered over the top of his *Oakmont County Weekly Gazette.*

The women grimaced a silent apology and tiptoed to the checkout counter to give Barbara the original. Within a few minutes she returned with four stacks. One for each lady and one for the library. She whispered, more like mimed 'good luck' with her lips and wiggled her fingers in goodbye.

Wanda organized the distribution. "I'll take Main Street. Hazel, why don't you take the square including the Medical Center and the fire and police stations? Oh, and don't forget Schiller and Smith attorneys across the way. Betty Sue, can you take these to the schools, since you know all the teachers, and also post one or two at the grocer's?"

"Sure, but I think Hazel should take Main. You need to take the Square, and probably make the police station your first stop. Todd is your nephew."

"You're right. I hope the mayor has chatted with Chief Brooks about it by now. It'll make my task a lot smoother." Wanda widened her eyes and crossed her fingers in a hopeful gesture then headed east.

She stopped at the steps to the police station, sucked in a breath of courage, and entered. Regan Weber, the new cadet, greeted her by name. Todd, having likely heard, dashed around the corner. "Aunt Wanda what are you doing here?"

She lifted her chin. "I am a citizen of this town. I have the right to come visit the local constabulary, don't I?"

He sputtered.

Regan stifled a giggle. Wanda wasn't sure it was due to her word usage to describe the police station or the flush on Todd's cheeks.

She wiped away the comment as if she swatted a pesky fly. "I'm kidding. Actually, I wanted to let y'all know about this." She peeled a flier off the stack and handed it to him. "We have already registered with the national office and have talked with a coordinator who is willing to drive down from Fort Worth tomorrow to meet with us." She couldn't help the proud tone in her voice. Wanda had to admit this project made her feel useful.

Todd leaned against the desk. He rubbed his head. "Wow. You've been busy. I think the chief will want to see this."

"Exactly why I came. I wanted him to know that we are distributing these around town. And of course, all of you are invited to attend. That goes without saying." She flashed a sweet smile to Regan.

"Wait here." He pumped his hand indicating she should

sit down in one of the plastic, designed-to-fit-nobody chairs.

She wiggled into one, pulling her skirt to her knees. Regan went back to whatever report she had been entering into the database.

A few minutes later, Chief Brooks emerged from his office, followed by a slightly nervous-looking Todd. He extended his hand. Wanda rose and took it in a similar confident grip as she had with the mayor.

"I just got off the phone with Mayor Porter. He told me you had been to see him and discussed this matter. *He* seems to think it is a good idea."

"Does that mean you don't?"

The sound of Regan's fingers clicking on the keyboard halted. Todd cast his gaze to the acoustic ceiling tiles.

"Let's have a chat in my office." Chief Brooks waved his hand toward the door with his name printed on it. "Officer Martin, you may as well attend this meeting as well."

"Yes, sir." Todd gave his aunt a narrowed-eye glance and then followed behind her.

What was the big deal? Had she stepped on toes?

After she had been seated, the chief sat in his chair. It released a loud squeak as if in protest. Todd stood at semi-attention off to the left and, by his expression, chose to ignore the sound. Wanda did as well, almost. She coughed briefly into her fist to keep from laughing.

"Mrs. Warner, do you think our force is not doing an adequate job of protecting this community?" Chief Brooks set his jaw.

She opened her mouth, then closed it again. So, it had become personal? What an inflated male ego he demonstrated.

Wanda thought of her response long and hard. If she said yes, it would not fare well for her nephew. If she said no, then her cause had no teeth. Now she knew how Jesus felt before the Pharisees. But he had the upper hand knowing their hearts. She wasn't sure how to read Chief Brooks at the moment.

That's it. Go to the source. Remain neutral.

She reached into her purse for the information she had printed from the library computer and read it out loud. "The national organization's flier states the purpose of a neighborhood watch is to assist the police in the protection of personal property and to build a greater sense of community among neighbors. It raises respect for the police and is a positive influence on the youth." She held it out for him to take. "They suggest a town our size should have at least three teams of three to four each. I believe one should cover the homes south of Main, one cover north of Main as far as East and West Elm, and then one to include the houses up to Woodway Drive. Lakeview Apartments may want to form their own since there are 45 units."

Chief Brooks eyed the flier. "You think there will be that much of an interest?"

"If I didn't, sir, I wouldn't have spent the morning learning about it and organizing this. I already know of six people who are interested. The fliers are being distributed as we speak. We would love it if you came to the meeting, lent your advice, and met the organizer, an Officer McIntyre from the FWPD."

That got his attention. Of course, he would have to come. Especially if another law enforcement officer attended. Particularly if that officer drove the hour and half from Fort Worth.

Todd stuck his tongue in his cheek and gave his aunt a small wink.

Chief Brooks rose. "Very well. I will be there tomorrow morning at 9:45."

Wanda took it as a dismissal. She got up, extended her hand, and wondered if she should have brought a peace pipe from the Oakmont County Museum. Except she didn't smoke. She hoped the chief didn't either. Though he did fit the image of a man who liked a big stogie.

As she walked down the hall to the exit, Todd rushed ahead to hold the front door open for her.

"Sunday, over Scrabble, you are going to explain to me what this is really all about."

She fluttered her eyelashes. "I have no idea what you mean."

His sigh hit her ears as she scooted past him.

CHAPTER SIX

To Wanda's delight, by 9:54 the next morning, the stragglers could barely scoot into Priscilla's to find room to stand. Office McIntyre took a position near the counter after Sally, Priscilla's sister and owner of Sally's Salads, found a wooden produce box for him to stand upon. He wore a wireless mike, courtesy of Pastor Bob from Holy Hill Church where Wanda worshipped.

Wanda, Evelyn, and Betty Sue spent the previous evening making blueberry bran muffins. Hazel brought two dozen freshly made doughnuts donated by the Grocery Mart to accompany Priscilla's famous cinnamon rolls. The ladies passed the trays and boxes through the crowd as Sally and Priscilla poured coffee into disposable cups.

At one minute past, Evelyn whistled with her fingers to her teeth. Half the room stopped chatting. Then Pastor Bob yelled out, "The Lord be with you."

Murmurs of "also with you" filtered through as everyone bowed their heads.

His gentle but booming voice lifted the meeting into

God's hands, and then Wanda introduced the police officer. "We would like to thank Officer Douglas McIntyre for driving in from Fort Worth this morning."

Approving mumbles waved through the gathering. Chief Brooks inched his way to the front and shook the officer's hand, giving a small speech of gratitude. Then Mayor Porter, not to be upstaged, reiterated the same sentiments, and told Office McIntyre about their wonderful, law-abiding town . . . for the next ten minutes.

Finally, the policeman stepped up onto the box and began. "Many of you may have heard of a neighborhood watch. But I am here to tell you why it is beneficial and how to start one. It is a well-known fact that watches not only help reduce crime, but they promote community awareness, renew camaraderie between neighbors, and have a positive influence on the youth, who are less likely to experiment with drugs, underage drinking, and reckless behaviors."

Betty Sue, as a retired teacher began to clap, and several of the current high school teachers joined in, along with Fred Ballinger. Wanda noticed Beverly Newby, owner of Anna's Antiques, nodding in agreement.

"I am sure everyone here respects and appreciates the fine police force you have here. However, it is even more solidified when citizens and police cooperate in a neighborhood watch formation and maintenance."

Samuel Schiller, one of the local attorneys, raised his hand. "How do we do that?"

"Good question." The policeman smiled. "We would

recommend you have at least three groups with three to four members in each. Mrs. Warner has a fact sheet and sign-up sheet on the back table by the door. Each member simply patrols their designated area on a rotation basis, especially at night. Each team has a captain who can be contacted if anyone in the neighborhood detects unusual activity. So, as you see, the whole town becomes involved. Even if you do not want to be a patroller, you can still participate. The captains hold regular meetings and communicate often with the police department. Captains can also organize food drives, holiday neighborhood parties, cleanup crews, etc."

"You are saying that these watches are designed to not only protect us but bring us closer together?" Beverly stood on tiptoes to be seen.

The officer acknowledged her. "Exactly. The more you know your neighbors, the easier it will be to not only know if they need assistance of any kind but what is or is not unusual behavior."

Mr. Baker dashed his gaze to the ground as several eyes landed on him. Wanda felt her cheeks heat. How many times should she apologize to the poor man? Maybe she'd take him another casserole. And a few cans of cat food.

Carl Smithers, who owned the gas station and used car lot, raised his hand. "Do we carry guns?"

Chief Brooks face paled.

"No." Officer McIntyre shook his head firmly. "Neighborhood watch patrols are only to inform, not perform, that is instigate any actions that may seem heroic.

I cannot emphasize that fact enough."

"Who screens the reports for pertinence? I mean, this town, like every small town I'm sure, has a few, well . . . busybodies." Aurora's eyes narrowed on Wanda.

Wanda harrumphed. How dare she? Then she caught Pastor Bob's fatherly glare and bit her lip. Betty Sue patted her arm and Evelyn gave her a sympathetic smile. Wanda calmed her breathing and instead of reacting, thanked God for good friends who loved and supported her.

Sally spoke next. "Can women patrol, or should only men?"

Officer McIntyre cleared his throat. "Women have been effective, but I'd suggest, at the risk of sounding chauvinistic, that the men would probably be the best defense after dark. I wouldn't mind my wife driving around in a locked car, but I wouldn't want her on foot no matter how safe our neighborhood seemed."

Rumbles of opinions floated through the crowd.

"Do you have any children?" Barbara Mills always had a heart for kids, especially those just learning to read.

The officer blushed. "Um, yes. Two. My son is eight and my daughter is six." He scanned the café. "Anyone else?"

Beverly raised her hand. "I run an antique store in town. Anna's Antiques, named after my dear grandmother who collected Victorian pieces. I have never had any troubles but should I install an alarm?"

He scratched his head. "It is always a wise plan. Talk

to your insurance agent to see if it will help lower your premiums, too."

She giggled. "Well, that would be easy." She twisted and pointed. "It's my son-in-law, Jay King. Jay, why haven't you told me about this?"

He opened his mouth, then shut it again, with an expression of perplexity on his face as if she'd asked him if he was still beating his wife. There was no right answer.

Chuckles rippled through the room.

McIntyre came to the rescue. "Anyone else have questions . . . about neighborhood watches?"

Murmurs and head shakes answered him back.

After a few seconds, Wanda took the mike from his lapel and spoke into it before the Mayor could begin another speech. She thanked him for his visit. Hazel presented him with a small bouquet of roses, and Betty Sue gave him a box of breakfast breads to take home.

Everyone applauded. When the noise subsided, Wanda announced that the organization of teams would take place Tuesday evening at seven o'clock in the Holy Hill Church fellowship hall. Big B Barbecue would provide dinner. Captains would be voted on at that time.

The meeting ended a little after eleven. Evelyn, Betty Sue, and Wanda lingered to help Priscilla clean up.

"I think that went really well." Betty Sue grinned as she wiped muffin crumbs from the tables.

Wanda's chest swelled with pride. "Maybe people in this town will now understand I only have everyone's best interests at heart."

Evelyn scoffed. "Well, most will. I could not believe Aurora's comment."

"Forgive and forget." Betty Sue squeezed her arm. "That is what we are called to do, even if the other person won't."

"Yes, but it is hard. I so wanted to stuff a doughnut in her pie hole." Wanda sniffed.

The ladies crowed. Until they noticed Pastor Bob had returned.

"Oh, sorry Pastor Bob." Wanda lowered her eyes to the broom in her hands.

"Confession is good for the soul." He gave her a warm smile. "I forgot to tell you. The day care council is also meeting Tuesday evening. They usually meet on the fourth Tuesday of the month but postponed it last week when we were under that tornado warning."

"Will that be a problem?" Wanda stopped sweeping.

"I doubt it. They can meet in my office. Just wanted you to know." He tipped his hand to his forehead. "Ladies. Thank you for organizing this."

He snatched a cup of coffee, left two dollars on the counter, and walked out whistling "Ye Watchers and Ye Holy Ones," an old English hymn from the early 1900's.

Todd arrived at Wanda's house at 10:40 Sunday morning. "Walk or ride?"

"Ride. It's already eighty degrees out there and the humidity is about the same. If we hoofed it, I'd look like a piece of lettuce left out overnight by the time we get there."

He chuckled and closed the door behind them. She handed him the keys to her Hyundai, not wishing to crawl into his sardine can of a sports car. He clicked the fob and then opened the passenger door for her.

"I hear there was quite a turnout yesterday at Sally's. The chief chatted about it off and on all afternoon. Made it mandatory for all police officials to be available on Tuesday evening at the church."

"All four of you?" Wanda winked.

He ignored her. "So why the sudden interest in a neighborhood watch?"

"To exonerate me in the community. And to give me some credence, I guess. I want people to know I have this town's best interests in my heart. I'm not a busybody."

He turned the corner. "Despite what some lady who lives by the lake says?"

"Oh, so you heard?"

"Aunt Wanda. It's my job to hear."

She shifted her attention to the passenger side window. "And not mine, right?"

"I didn't say that. The four of us cannot be everywhere, even in a community of 472 souls."

She gasped. "Ester Mae had her baby?"

"In the wee hours this morning. A girl. Six pounds, eleven ounces. They are naming her Lucy."

"Aw. Well, we will have to organize meals."

He took his hand from the steering wheel long enough to squeeze her shoulder. "That's my aunt."

They pulled into the parking lot, and he circled to find a spot closer to the main entrance. As he opened her car door and held a hand for her to exit, he whispered into her ear. "I know this has to do with what I told you might be happening in this area. Do not, I repeat, *do not* let anyone else know. I mean it, Aunt Wanda. It might cost me my badge."

She made a zipped motion across her mouth and walked ahead of him up the steps into the church. She prayed that neither Betty Sue nor Evelyn had told anyone. Or Sally . . . Hazel . . .

Surely not.

Holy Hill's education sessions were ending and people piled into the hallway between the sanctuary and the fellowship hall. Some had been to the earlier service, others were grabbing a cup of coffee to swallow down before attending the eleven o'clock one.

Ray O'Malley, the owner of the Hook & Owl Irish Pub cornered Todd. "What's the word on the thieves, man? I don't want my till hit."

"Yeah, have you spotted them? You were on duty the past two nights, right?" Carl Smithers edged into the group of men now surrounding Todd.

Wanda dashed to the women's restroom.

CHAPTER SEVEN

The fact that today's sermon was on being neighborly without being nosy didn't help matters. And when Pastor Bob alluded to the fact that he encouraged the neighborhood watch, especially in lieu of the recent robbery up the way in Burleson, whose burglars were still not apprehended, Wanda sank in her pew.

Todd didn't speak to her all the way home. Wanda blinked tears from her eyes. He twisted his head to her, a scowl still visible, as he edged into her driveway.

"Todd, I am so sorry. I didn't think . . ."

"Obviously." He got out, slammed the driver-side door, and rounded the back to let her out.

She pleaded with her most sincere, I-love-you dear-boy face. "What can I do to make up for this?"

He leaned against the post to her back porch stairs. His facial features suddenly aged ten years. Deep furrows spread across his brow. "It's bound to have gotten back to the chief by now. Why I haven't gotten a call, I don't know. Maybe he is waiting until Monday to fire me."

She opened her kitchen door. "You're overreacting. Come, sit down. I'll pour you a tall glass of iced tea and fix you an egg salad sandwich."

"Not in the mood, Aunt Wanda. Sorry. I better go."

"What about our Scrabble game?" She pointed to the top of the refrigerator.

"Maybe later. I'll call you."

Wanda watched him leave, his head low and footsteps heavy. What had she done? Why did her good intentions always seem to backfire?

She closed the kitchen door with a soft click and slumped into the kitchen chair for a good cry and an urgent prayer.

Then she washed her face and texted Evelyn.

Her neighbor tapped on the back door fifteen minutes later. "Whatcha need?"

"A friend, advice, and maybe a spanking."

Evelyn lifted one of her penciled-in eyebrows. "Start at the beginning."

She did, and then began to sniffle once more.

Evelyn wrapped her in a hug. "There is still time to do damage control. Tomorrow morning march down to that police station and tell Chief Brooks it is all your fault. You jumped to the conclusion that the burglars must be around here because of the vacant Ferguson House. Which, given time, you would have. Especially after what Aurora said."

She dabbed her eyes with a dish towel. "Okay. I'll do that. Should I tell Todd?"

"Yeah, I would."

After Evelyn left, Wanda did two loads of laundry, pulled some weeds out of her begonia bed, and practiced what she'd say to the chief in the morning. She then decided to call Todd.

He listened. "Thanks, Aunt Wanda. But I don't want you to fib."

"I won't be. Not really. As Evelyn said, I'd have come to that conclusion anyway. If they abandoned their van near Alvarado, it only makes sense they'd head down the railroad tracks to here. No way they'd go to Keene or Cleburne. Too many people."

"Okay. Say, why don't I run by Better Burgers and bring you dinner tonight about seven. We can finish our game then."

Warmth spread from her heart down her arms. He'd forgiven her. "Make it six. That British murder mystery series is on PBS at seven. I know you don't like cop shows."

"You got that right."

"Okay, then. I'll see you a little after six. I'd like the steak fingers with country gravy, fries, and Texas Toast. Wanna split some onion rings?"

So much for her slightly bulging waistline.

He arrived right on time. The Warner trait for

punctuality, one her sister's husband had never learned. Now she, and the rest of the family knew why he often showed up late. The snake. She thanked the heavens that Todd had turned out right.

Wanda's stomach growled at the wonderful aromas seeping through the takeout sacks as he emptied the contents onto her table. She filled two tumblers with sun-brewed iced tea then sat down in anticipation.

Her eyes rolled in delight as she bit into a still-warm onion ring. The steak fingers were seasoned just right, the gravy creamy and thick with the right amount of peppercorns. Wanda had toyed with the idea of eating half tonight and refrigerating the rest for tomorrow's lunch. But fries rarely held their crispness. And the food tasted way too good when hot and fresh.

She'd walk a mile tomorrow. Maybe two. Early, before the temps rose above eighty. Maybe check out that beginners' Zumba class, too.

After they were both too stuffed to move, Wanda and Todd resumed their Scrabble game. They'd just played the words cave, bushes, auto, and shot when Todd's cell phone rang. He excused himself from the table and took the call.

Wanda could only hear his voice, not anything being said. After a minute or so he came back into the kitchen. His face held a seriousness that made her neck chill.

"What's wrong? Can you tell me?"

"Why not? It'll be all over town by sunrise." He rubbed his forehead. "Carl Smithers decided to start his own patrol tonight."

Wanda sighed. Carl wanted to be the first at everything so he'd get the glory.

Todd continued, "Unfortunately he brought his deer rifle. He saw a figure dashing into the woods behind the Ferguson place, jumped the fence and followed. Shot the guy at the clearing by the lake."

"Oh my. Is he . . ."

"Yeah. At the scene. Carl's being booked. I better go."

He left. Wanda eased into the kitchen chair unsure of what to do—if anything. Then she glanced at the board where Todd had just played the word "shot" off her word "auto." Carl repaired and sold autos.

Coincidence? Hardly.

Another shiver danced up her spine. She covered the board with a towel and slid it back on top of the fridge. Then she texted Evelyn and Betty Sue to come over . . . *NOW*.

Julie B Cosgrove

CHAPTER EIGHT

Betty Sue's face froze in a half-shocked, half-curious pose. Evelyn reported that half the town had already trekked up to Woodway, only to be turned away by not only the town's policemen but the county sheriff's patrol arriving on the scene.

"How do you know this?"

Evelyn shrugged. "I have my sources."

Wanda handed her a tumbler of unsweetened iced tea and Betty Sue one with two packets of stevia stirred in, the way Betty Sue liked it. She also knew her best friend liked thin crust pizza with spinach, mushrooms, and bacon, and that at sixty-four she was a closet Toby Mac fan, and she had a mild heartthrob for one of the detectives on a British mystery series. The same one Wanda watched on PBS. She also knew where Betty Sue hid her diaries from high school and college and remembered most of the content of her prayer journals. After all, they had been friends since third grade, gone on double dates in high school, and been each other's honor attendants at their weddings.

Wanda knew less about Evelyn, the newcomer, who had only lived there about ten years or so. Her favorite dish was the Irish stew at the Hook & Owl, which she stated to be just like her grandmother's recipe from the old country. A Hank Williams fan, she had most of his albums and CD's, and she was widowed in the Shock and Awe era in her thirties, never remarrying.

Betty Sue sat across from her. "She was over at Hazel's, pumping her for more info on the Ferguson place when things went down. That's the correct term isn't it?" She passed her gaze to Evelyn.

"Yes. My late husband always said you learn a lot if you let people talk. They will develop a trust if they can lead the conversation and then will open up more." She scooted forward in her chair. "Hazel has been wondering if she had been imagining things or not. Twice this week, for no apparent reason, she woke from a sound sleep, and looked out her bedroom window. It is on the second floor and is angled to where you can see the both the front and back of the Ferguson place when the trees have not quite leafed out."

"What did she see?" Wanda leaned in closer.

"Tonight, or in the past night?"

Wanda and Betty Sue said, "Both," in unison.

"Well," Evelyn settled back with a dramatic pause and took a long gulp of tea.

Betty Sue rubbed her nose, a nervous habit she had developed early in life when allergies plagued her. She'd outgrown most of them.

"When she gazed out her window on the first night, she thought she saw someone scooting through the back lawns to the woods. But then again it could have been the tree limbs moving in the breeze."

"I thought the same thing Friday night as I walked Sophie."

"Really? Well, the second night, she was more certain she saw a man at the edge of the woods, but he disappeared back in them before she got a good look."

"Did she tell the police?" Betty Sue rubbed her nose again.

"She saw a police car turning onto 8th from Oak and ran downstairs to wave it over." Evelyn's eyes shifted to Wanda. "It was Todd's shift."

"And he never said a word."

"Why would he, Wanda? Nothing came of it. She said he called her later the next morning to tell her he had driven by several more times and never noticed anything out of the ordinary."

"What about tonight? What did y'all see?"

"We were on her back patio enjoying the fireflies and a cup of cinnamon vanilla latte from her fancy brewer when we heard the shot echo. Boom. We both stared at each other, wondering the same thing. Gunfire? Outside of hunting season?"

"What did you do?" Betty Sue grabbed a paper napkin and dabbed her nose in earnest.

"We dashed back inside, of course. By the time we went to peer through her living room bay window, we could hear the sirens and see the squad car lights. Didn't you two hear a thing?"

"I had the TV on. I watch the PBS murder mysteries on Sunday nights." Betty Sue dipped her head like a teenage girl confessing she liked a boy in her class. "That detective is kinda cute. Something about his accent. I like the dog, too."

The other two ladies nodded.

"Earlier, Todd and I were playing Scrabble while chomping on onion rings and fries from Better Burger then he got a call and told me Carl had shot the guy." She waggled her finger. "Don't give me that disgusted look Betty Sue. For your information, I also had steak fingers with gravy and Texas Toast."

"Wanda, all that salt and carbs. Why, you'll bloat up like a pig on a skewer at a luau."

"Lovely image. Thanks."

Betty Sue swallowed some tea. "I worry about your diet."

"You mean that I am not constantly on one like you?"

"No." She slammed the glass down. "Because you are my dearest friend, and I want you to live a lot longer."

"Ladies." Evelyn held up her hands. "Back to the shooting?"

The two friends glanced at each other, mouthed the word 'sorry,' and then turned their attention back to Evelyn.

"Go on, Ev. What happened next?" Wanda leaned forward, focused on her friend's face.

"Well, then the police ran into the woods. And after the crowd began to gather, they roped off a section with that yellow tape. More cop cars arrived on the scene, one from Cleburne along with the county sheriff's truck. Drove right into the Ferguson driveway and across the back lawn. Then the county coroner's van showed up. About fifteen minutes later, as we were being shooed away from the curbs on 8th street, Carl Smithers came out handcuffed, led by Jimmy Bob, the other patrol officer in town, to the squad car. As they drove away, Todd helped wheel a body on a gurney out of the woods and into the van."

"Dead?" Betty Sue gasped.

"Yep. Unless they now zip people in black bags for some sort of weird oxygen treatment."

Betty Sue scrunched her nose.

Wanda stifled a chuckle. "And that's it?"

"That's it. Everyone dispersed and went home." Evelyn folded her hands in her lap like a final punctuation mark.

"You think it was one of the thieves?" It had to be. That was the most logical thought. At least, the most logical to Wanda.

"Well, that would make the most sense. Don't ya think?" Evelyn harrumphed. "I figure they got antsy hiding out. One tried to sneak out of the woods, but Carl spotted him."

"Or maybe one of them wanted the jewelry all for

himself and tried to leave with it. So, Carl saw him running, thought he was escaping, and shot him, thinking he was doing his duty. You know how he is. Always wants to be the big shot." Betty Sue put her hand to her mouth when she realized her pun.

Evelyn turned to Wanda. "She does have a point."

The three remained silent for a few moments.

Then Wanda sucked in a breath.

"What?" Evelyn pushed her eyebrows together.

"The Scrabble words. The set with jewels and escape and perp? The others were "lying" and "woods" so I thought it meant the house lying near the woods, not a body lying in the woods. Or is it laying?"

Her friends both stared at her.

She waved the thought away like a gnat buzzing her face. "Anyway, tonight when we continued the game. Look what we spelled." She grabbed the board from its perch on top of the fridge and removed the dish towel cover.

Betty Sue rubbed her hands together. "Well, well. Look at that. Bushes, shot, cave, auto. Hmmm. I get bushes and shot. But there are no caves around here, are there? And auto?'

"I don't recall any stories about caves growing up." Wanda titled her head to read the board again. "Maybe it has a double meaning?"

"Or this is all a coincidence. Doesn't the Bible say something about being wary of the devil's schemes?" Evelyn crossed her arms.

"True. But we were playing an innocent word game not having a seance."

Betty Sue let out a small gasp. "Wanda, you think Todd is wondering the same thing?"

She shook her head. "I honestly don't know. But I don't think I am going to get much sleep tonight."

"No one is." Evelyn ran her hands up and down her arms.

Wanda resisted the urge to do the same, though goose pimples were beginning to coat her shoulders. "Why? Because we rarely have a shooting?"

"Well, there is that. But I'm wondering." Evelyn sighed. "There were three burglars, right? Where are the other two?"

Betty Sue didn't answer. Wanda had no idea either, but the sensation of someone tiptoeing over her grave began again.

No make that more like Fred Astaire and Ginger Rogers tap dancing on it.

Julie B Cosgrove

CHAPTER NINE

Wanda stayed up late, but Todd never called. She figured booking Carl, getting his statement, and whatever else they did, took time. He probably was still at it or decided it was too late to disturb her.

She lay awake staring at the shadows on the ceiling caused by the breeze tickling the tree limbs. The food lay like a pallet of bricks in her gut, but the word play choices swirled in her brain like cotton candy being made on a stick at the county fair.

Another fact stuck in her thoughts. The two had played these words in order of the events. Weird. Did "cave" and "auto" relate to events yet to come?

She threw off the covers and grabbed her phone to text Todd. *Heard about the shooting. Matches some of our last Scrabble words. Don't you agree?*

Go to sleep, Aunt Wanda. We'll talk over lunch tomorrow. Sally's at 1?

Ok. Goodnight.

She huffed out a long sigh and decided to read some of

the Psalms. She had made a pact with her Bible study group to read one a day for the next seven weeks, beginning with the first. Then each week, they'd discuss what they had read.

Sophie hopped up her doggy stairs at the foot of the bed and settled in with her.

"What? You want me to read them out loud?" She stroked her pup's velvety floppy ears. She began with Psalm 7, where David thanks God for His protection and provisions. Then she stopped when she read,

> *Lord my God, if I have done this and there is guilt on my hands—if I have repaid my ally with evil or without cause have robbed my foe—then let my enemy pursue and overtake me; let him trample my life to the ground and make me sleep in the dust.*

Huh? Betty Sue's scenario floated through her head. Had one of the thieves tried to steal from the others and sneak off into the night, only to be caught and shot by Carl? She shook it off and kept reading.

The next verses were all about God coming to David's aid and defeating his enemies, a common theme in the psalms. Then began another strange set of verses.

> *Whoever is pregnant with evil conceives trouble and gives birth to disillusionment. Whoever digs a hole and scoops it out falls into the pit they have made. The trouble they cause recoils on them; their violence comes*

down on their own heads.

Wanda set the Bible down. The only one in town who had been pregnant was Ester Mae. No way. She had the voice of an angel, could play the organ like no one's business, and was as squeaky clean as they come. Besides, she'd had her baby. It had to mean something else.

Wanda scanned the words again. Uh, oh.

Is that what *she* was doing? Was she spreading disillusionment? Did word of forming a neighborhood watch somehow get back to the thieves and spook them?

Had her good intentions gotten Carl so riled up that he took action into his own hands in an attempt to gain favor from the community? Had she unknowingly brought violence down on Scrub Oak's head?

Bible study was at ten in the morning. Dare she bring this up? Or would they all look at her weird? Maybe she should meet with her pastor first.

After a night of restlessness, Wanda decided that an extra strong coffee and a bit of common sense was in order. She dug the bag of Kenyan coffee from the back of the pantry. Hazel had given it to her and to each of the other members of the beautification committee for Christmas in a Santa mug along with a candy cane. Roses were not blooming then of course.

One sip and her brain shuddered awake, along with her taste buds. Wow. She added three scoops of sugar then grabbed the half and half from the fridge and filled her mug to the rim. Better.

Ten after seven. Sophie whimpered and pawed the backdoor to be let out. Wanda stood on the porch and watched her pet with one eye, the other taking in her neighborhood. All seemed as quiet as it had every morning in Scrub Oak. The sun started its climb into the sky, the sparrows and finches tweeted and fluttered in the old oak tree before pecking at the feeder. Old Mr. Keller's morning hacking cough echoed off the roof tops as he no doubt bent to retrieve his Dallas newspaper thrown into the bushes, par usual. The Patterson's basset hound sounded his low-toned ruffs as he greeted someone walking by. Life back to normal.

Except that there had been a shooting and one of the town's high-ranking citizens, at least in his own estimation, sat in a jail cell. That sort of thing didn't happen every day in Scrub Oak. She still felt a twinge of guilt that somehow, she had instigated it.

She didn't get to speak to Pastor Bob about it. He was visiting the sick. But the ladies in her Bible study consoled her. Beverly Newby patted her shoulder. "Your intentions were good. It is not your fault Carl decided to take matters into his own hands. That officer was very clear about not carrying guns."

Several of the ladies nodded as they peered over their

reading glasses. A heaviness lifted from Wanda's chest. Then it sank back in. "But Carl's intentions were probably good, too."

"Well," Kathy King, Beverly's daughter, raised both eyebrows. "Carl is known to do stuff to gain attention."

Scoffing chuckles could be heard around the room.

"Good morning, Ladies." Pastor Bob, back from his rounds, entered and gave a nod to each of them. "Wanda, I like your idea of reading through the Psalms. When we really dig in, God can nudge us through His word. He gives us discernment, but it does take courage to act on what He shows us. Shall we stop and pray for the events of last night? For Carl, the police, and even the family of the man who was killed?"

Shuffling occurred as the women bowed their heads. But during the prayer and the rest of the Bible study, a growing desire began to bloom in Wanda's heart.

At first, she dismissed it as trying to ease her own conscience. But then again, something did not add up. What or why, she couldn't tell. More than a feeling, but not quite an idea. It hung in her thoughts like an opaque curtain obscuring the clear truth.

One thing she did know, though. Deep inside she believed Carl to be wrongly accused. She'd known him when he was the shy kid in high school afraid of having his head dunked in the toilets. But how to go about proving it without making the police, especially Todd, look like small town buffoons?

Maybe after she talked to Todd over lunch and got more details, the curtain would open to reveal the way she must proceed. She packed up her Bible and notebook and headed out. An hour and a half to kill. Go back home, or snoop around town? Part of her wanted to check out the woods, but if the other two burglars still hid out in them, well, that would be a stupid thing to do. Camping out in Aurora's backyard wasn't an option. That woman's lacquered gel nails would be clicking on her latest iPhone faster than Wanda could say lickety-split.

Rent one of the cabins at the Woodway Resort? She, Evelyn, and Betty Sue could take turns keeping watch. She pulled up their website on her phone. What, $250 a night? Well, they advertised two bedrooms with lake access, but still. Sheesh.

She could wander into Anna's Antiques and talk to Beverly some more. Scope out the place and see if she really had anything of great value in there. People opened up to Beverly, so maybe she had gleaned more information. If not, Wanda would peruse the aisles of the grocery store, catch the gist of a few conversations, and maybe pick up a few items she'd never tried before.

With a plan in hand, Wanda's steps lightened and quickened the three blocks to Anna's. As she entered the shop, the soft tinkling of the old fashion bell on the door along with a welcomed blast of air-conditioning greeted her. Then Beverly's wonderful smile.

"Wanda. What a pleasure. I barely made it back to the

shop in time to open."

"I wanted to thank you for your kind words in Bible study this morning."

A soft blush, the color of the Victorian divan in the corner of the shop, colored Beverly's cheeks. "Psfft. Don't mention it."

Wanda wandered to the counter. "Well, I still feel somewhat responsible for stirring the hornet's nest."

"It was chock full of hornets anyway. You know how Carl is." She poured a cup of iced water from a pitcher sweating on a sterling silver tray. "Here you are. The heat is already close to unbearable."

Wanda took a long, grateful gulp. "Have you noticed Carl being more agitated than normal lately? I am trying to figure out what possessed him to jump the gun." She stopped and raised her hand to her mouth. "You know what I mean."

Beverly's laugh reminded Wanda of a wind chime in the summer breeze. She poured herself a glass and took a sip before responding as if she wanted to weigh her words first.

Wanda waited.

"Well, now that you mention it." She wiped both corners of her mouth with an embroidered lace hankie retrieved from her sleeve. "He cornered Chief Brooks last week on the sidewalk right near my stoop. I had the door open after that nice rain to air out the shop, so I couldn't help but overhear."

"Naturally."

"Something about a suspected attempt to steal one of his used cars last Tuesday evening?"

"What did Chief Brooks say?"

"I don't remember, exactly. It was more his tone. I recall back on the ranch when I was about ten, Papa had a stubborn colt who would not let anyone approach him. Papa spent days sweet talking him in a calm, even manner until the little jittery horse finally responded and came to eat a sugar cube from his hand. That's what it reminded me of."

"Hmm. I see. So perhaps Carl became antsy, thinking the burglars were out to snatch a getaway car."

She said it more as a statement to herself. Wanda finished her water and thanked Beverly. Then she headed to the police station to persuade Chief Brooks into letting her speak with Carl. Perhaps the same calm manner of persuasion would work on the chief. What's good for the goose . . . as they say.

"Absolutely not." Chief Brooks' thundering voice bounced off the low ceiling and around the main room of the police station.

"But, Chief Brooks, it is only for a minute. I can't help but take some responsibility for his actions." She glanced down at her hands and sniffled.

The police chief coughed into his fist and took a step back. Good. Seeing a woman get emotional typically unnerved him. Out of the corner of her eye she detected his jaw soften.

"Okay. But what transpires must be recorded in front of a police officer. Jim Bob, set up the examination room."

Wanda thanked him with as sweet a little-old-lady smile as she could muster and sat on the bench to wait. She glanced around the room and her eyes fell on a notice on the bulletin board to the right. A modern "wanted poster" of sorts briefly described the three robbers as captured by the jewelry store's security camera. From the fuzzy picture, she couldn't make out any facial details. They wore all black and had on makeshift black masks. One seemed taller, one stockier, and one, by his stature, appeared to be older. The ringleader? No pun intended.

She squinted to read more. Fingerprints had been found inside of a glove discarded in the dumpster two doors down. They belonged to a Butch McClain, whoever he was.

Wanda scoffed. Dumb move on Butch's part at any rate. She pulled out her phone, called up the internet, and keyed in his name in the search bar of the Texas Department of Public Safety's criminal lookup website. There she discovered that he was on parole for armed robbery of an antique coin shop in Weatherford in 2002. Bingo.

But had he been the one that Carl shot? How would she find out? Maybe wiggle it out of Todd? Perhaps not. She skated on thin ice with him as it was. And if he saw her here in the police station? His attitude wouldn't exactly melt that ice.

He wouldn't come on duty until the afternoon, since he usually took the later shift, leaving the early one for Jim Bob who had a family. The clock showed 10:45. Plenty of time, even if he waltzed in early to do paperwork.

"Mrs. Warner?" Jim Bob appeared and beckoned her with his finger. He held the door open to a sparse room with a rectangular, metal table surrounded by four folding chairs, similar to the ones they used in the Holy Hill fellowship hall. Carl sat with a scowl on his face, slumped into one of the chairs on the other side of the table. His hands remained on the table, cuffed with plastic ties.

Jim Bob motioned for her to sit on the near side and closed the door. He punched the tape recorder button. "I believe you two know each other. But for the record, Mrs. Wanda Lee Warner of Spruce Drive has requested five minutes with the suspect, Carl Smithers, owner of Carl's Used Cars."

Wanda swiveled around as her eyes widened. "Five minutes? That's all?"

Carl let out a sinister snicker. "Talk fast, Wanda. Whatcha need to know?"

She barely had time to think. Why had she not gone over sample questions in her head? "Um, I guess I wanted to know why you decided to go on patrol before we had formally organized a neighborhood watch?"

He stared at his cuffs. After a long second, he spoke

without glancing at her as if ashamed. "The neighborhood watch had nothing to do with it. I told the chief last week I suspected my cars were being cased. He blew it off. So, I have been prowling the streets since then on the lookout for any strangers. Haven't slept in five days."

Then she noticed the dark, sallow circles and drawn cheeks. Sleep-deprived and on edge, the man had snapped and acted hastily. Surely the judge would take that into account.

"I was eager to get this neighborhood watch going so I could get some shut-eye. I have nothing against your efforts, Wanda. You're in no way to blame."

Then his eyes slowly raised to meet hers. Did she detect a new cynicism she'd never seen before?

Gazing back, she questioned her instincts. One thing she did know, if Carl was innocent, it was up to her to prove it. The police obviously thought they had their man.

"I understand. Thank you for speaking with me." She tried to send him a mental message that she would help. With the tape recorder softly whirring and capturing every sound, it seemed the only way to communicate her plan.

Carl's eyes narrowed for a split second. A slight nod followed. Then Jim Bob announced that their time was up.

Wanda stood. "I hope I can visit you again in a few days."

The prisoner wet his lips. Did he get her drift?

She certainly hoped so.

Jim Bob escorted her out of the room, just as Todd

strolled down the hall from the backdoor where the squad car parking lot stood.

Oh, boy.

CHAPTER TEN

Wanda held up both hands to stop Todd from responding. "I came to see Carl. With the chief's permission."

He slowed his pace and grumbled an okay as he passed by her.

Obviously, things still remained icy between them. Wanda felt her heart crunch. Would he cancel on her for lunch? She hoped not. Somehow, she had to juggle proving Carl's intentions were not criminal while saving her nephew's face.

The clock over the police station desk showed 11:10. Almost two hours. That gave her time to do two things. Pray, and then recruit Betty Sue and Evelyn to assist her. Maybe if they worked together, it wouldn't seem as much of a slap for her nephew.

She stopped and stared at a flock of sparrows darting to a sprawling oak tree in the courthouse square. Who was she kidding? Everyone would figure out she was the ringleader.

She needed guidance. She walked up the block back to

Holy Hill church and slipped inside the sanctuary. The place oozed peace. Dark woods smelled of lemon oil. The sunlight streaming through the stained glassed windows laced the pews with soft colors like a celestial veil. A still coolness embraced her shoulders in a welcoming hug. She slipped into one of the back pews and closed her eyes. Maybe she'd get some divine inspiration.

A Bible lay open on the pew. It was turned to Ephesians 6. She scrunched her forehead as she picked it up and scanned it. The twenty-first verse caught her attention. *Tychicus, the dear brother and faithful servant in the Lord, will tell you everything, so that you also may know how I am and what I am doing.*

Her breath hitched. That was it. She'd keep Todd posted on anything she discovered and let him take the glory. Her heart became pounds lighter.

Pastor Bob entered from the side and began walking down the center aisle. "Wanda, may I help you?" His strong, baritone voice echoed off the rafters.

She grinned. "No, Pastor Bob. God just has. Thanks."

She scurried to gather her purse and scooted out of the pew. But as she pressed the large wooden door open, she turned to see her minister reading the Bible left open on the pew and scratching his head.

Oh, well. She'd explain it to him one day. Not now, though. Wanda texted Evelyn since it was her friend's preferred means of communication. Betty Sue always wanted a phone call. She asked them both to meet her at the

Coffee Bean at noon. That would give her time to surf a bit more about Butch McClain on the public computer at the library. Barbara wouldn't mind her using it this time of the day. The kids were all still in school. Much better than squinting at her small phone screen or dashing back home. That would be a waste of time.

Luckily, the library windows faced south so the sun didn't beat in. The temperature inside felt great. She wiggled her fingers at Barbara behind the checkout counter and pointed to the table with the computer.

The librarian smiled and nodded as she processed the books from the return bin.

Wanda passed Fred at one of the wooden tables. He glanced up from the newspaper spread out in front of him and silently greeted her. Nice man. She had caught him gazing a tad too long at Betty Sue during the fellowship coffee hour several times, but not in an inappropriate manner. More like in a sweet, high school crush sort of way. They had worked together on the school board for decades, but back then, both were married. Now both widowed, she wondered if perhaps . . .

Enough meddling. She had some investigating to do.

She booted up the computer, following the instructions posted on the monitor. Within a few minutes she found an article about McClain and a picture. Bingo.

Wanda zoomed the grainy online photo to 250 percent and studied the facial features as best she could. He appeared to be in his mid-forties. A harshness outlined his jawline and his eyes squinted like a sewer rat's. Of course, that might be a reaction to the camera flash. Did cameras still flash? Surely, they did. The one on her phone worked that way at night. But then again, she didn't take that many night pictures . . .

Oh Wanda, concentrate. Her mind bounced from thought to thought a lot lately. She had to focus. She copied and pasted the photo onto a new document and hit print so she could bring it up at the neighborhood watch meeting the next evening. She could show it to Todd and ask if this resembled the corpse in the morgue at the medical center. At least she assumed they had a morgue. The nearest funeral parlor was in Cleburne fifteen miles away. No way would the coroner take him there, right?

"Doing research?"

Fred's whisper made her jolt. She inhaled a long breath. "Fred, you made me jump out of my skin."

"Sorry." His face became penitent, almost like a puppy who had piddled on the oriental rug.

She gave him grace. "It's okay. I was at the police station earlier . . ."

"What for? Oh, yes, your nephew is on the force now. So glad to see him back in the fold, so to speak."

"Yes. Anyway, I saw a notice and it said one of the burglars of that jewelry heist in Burleson, Butch McClain, had a previous record of theft. I wanted to find out what I could and print his photo for the neighborhood watch groups, just in case."

He motioned if he could sit next to her. She agreed and he eased himself into the chair and leaned toward her ear to whisper. "I am so glad you thought about organizing one. I mean, Scrub Oak is still small, and we all know each other, but you never know. North Texas has jobs and land. Many folks from places like L.A. and Chicago are moving down here. Big city crime is bound to follow. I have been reading about it in an editorial in the *Dallas Times*." He hooked his thumb back to the table where he'd been sitting. "Carl told me about it and suggested I read it."

"Really?" Wanda swiveled to face him. "Maybe you'd like to address that tomorrow evening at the meeting. You are planning to attend, correct?"

"Um, yes." His cheeks became ruddy, which accented his soft blue eyes and white hair. "I suppose I could."

"Good."

He cocked his head to view the computer monitor. "Hey, that's the thief Carl mentioned. He knew he was out on parole and suspected he might be involved in the jewelry heist."

"Carl knew him?"

"Well, no. But he knew of him. Carl keeps up with this sort of stuff."

"I had no idea." Had Carl recognized Butch as the man in the woods and shot him?

"Shhhh." Barbara raised her finger to her lips.

Wanda sighed. She lowered her voice. "We'll chat later."

He winked, mouthed the word 'okay', and tiptoed back to his chair.

Yes, he and Betty Sue might make a good match . . . *stop. Back to Butch McClain.* She printed out a few more details about the Weatherford crime that had previously convicted him and then began to research if crime had indeed grown in the past year or so around the Metroplex. While most cities in Texas showed a decrease, Dallas, the biggest city in the area, showed the opposite. Not a comforting fact.

She typed in *crime report Fort Worth* in the search bar since it was the nearest large city and also where Officer McIntyre had jurisdiction. It pulled up the National Incident Based Reporting System (NIBRS) statistics. She downloaded the document and sent it to her email so she could print it out for people to have.

The clock on the lower left bar of the monitor showed 11:58. Already? She shut everything down, grabbed her photo of McClain, and waved goodbye to Fred and Barbara. She dashed to the grocer's, the sun already pounding on her back.

Wanda noticed Evelyn park her robin-egg blue Honda and called out to her, slightly out of breath. She really did have to join Betty Sue on her daily sunrise strolls more often. Betty Sue already waited inside and had commandeered a table.

"My, Wanda. You are perspiring. Have you been exercising?"

Wanda slid into a one of the bistro chairs and mopped her brow with one of the paper napkins from the chrome dispenser. "I have been walking all over downtown. Which is why I wanted to meet with you two. This morning I went to the police station and spoke to Carl."

"Do tell." Evelyn scooted in beside them.

Wanda recounted her events and conversations, with Carl, the chief, and with Fred in the library.

"Interesting." Betty Sue re-tucked her skirt around her legs. "But why call a meeting with us?"

Priscilla set down three tumblers of iced water. "What can I get for you ladies? I have a rich blend from a missionary in Uganda on special."

Wanda ordered an iced light roast latte with vanilla. Evelyn, with a heart for missions, decided to try the Ugandan special. Betty chose a green tea from Japan.

Wanda waited for Priscilla to go make their drinks then answered Betty Sue's question. "I looked in Carl's face. I honestly do not believe he meant to kill that guy. In fact, I think he may have recognized him as a burglar and shot at him to make him stop."

"You mean wound him in the leg or something so he couldn't run while Carl called the police?"

"Yes, Evelyn. I think so. But instead, he aimed too high." Wanda took a long gulp of the iced water just as Priscilla brought their orders.

"Make sense." Evelyn snorted. "Carl always loves to go deer hunting but he never lands one. I heard he has a horrid aim. Leave it to him to try and maim the guy and hit his heart instead."

"From whom, Evelyn?" Betty Sue wrinkled her button nose. She'd told Wanda before that she never could understand why men wanted to kill such graceful, gentle creatures.

"I don't recall. Around. He used to go shooting with Aurora's hubby."

Betty Sue gasped. "The one who was killed in a hunting accident last year?" She turned to Wanda. "You don't think Carl accidentally shot him, too, do you?"

Evelyn gazed at Wanda. "Do you?"

Wanda felt the blood slip from her face. "I, um . . . don't know. No one ever said."

CHAPTER ELEVEN

The latte sloshed in Wanda's gut as Betty Sue and Evelyn chatted about the article. Could Carl be a double murderer? Or just a really bad shot?

She would have to stealthily pry more information on that from Todd. Aurora's husband had been fatally shot while on a deer hunt in the first week of Todd's joining the force. She recalled that much vividly.

"But it was ruled an accident, right?" Wanda half-mumbled it to herself.

"What?" Evelyn glanced up from the mug shot. "Did you say something?"

"Aurora's husband. An accidental death."

"Yes. That is how they ruled it. Stray bullet from a careless hunter. So many come around here in the fall. No way to tell whose unless they did forensics on every shotgun in the county." Evelyn took a sip of her coffee. "Ugh. This could strip wallpaper."

"That's why I always stick to green tea. Plenty of caffeine, very little acidity. Antioxidants, too." Betty Sue raised her cup in a semi-toast.

"But it has no taste." Evelyn shuddered as she took another gulp of her brew.

"And that has too much."

Wanda half-heard them. She still mulled over the possibility of Carl killing . . . what had his name been? On the edge of her memory. Robert, perhaps. Pronounced *Ro-bear*. Yes, that was it.

He'd been Aurora's third husband, if she recalled correctly. The woman had always attracted men like gnats, even in high school. Prom queen, head cheerleader, crowned Miss Oakmont County two years in a row.

Betty Sue's laugh hit her ears. She waggled a finger at Wanda. "I know that expression. You are thinking about Aurora, aren't you?"

"Guilty."

"You two never got along. You the tomboy, she the princess."

Wanda felt a sudden penitence. "Still, no one deserves to lose a husband that way. We all know that."

The other two widows nodded and dropped their eyes. Evelyn's had been killed in war, and Betty Sue's died of prostate cancer. Wanda's beloved Big Bill, as everyone called him, had never come home from a business convention. He had a heart attack in the night, and the hotel chambermaid discovered him the next morning. Ten years ago.

"Maybe we should be more friendly to her. Invite her

for a Saturday brunch. It must get lonely in that chalet on the lake." Wanda pushed the rest of her iced latte away.

"Right. With her indoor Olympic-sized pool, fifty-inch TV, and piped-in music." Evelyn sniffed.

"How did you know that?"

"You told me, Wanda. When you were staking out the resort from her backyard and peeked in the windows."

"Oh, right."

Betty Sue patted Wanda's hand. "You have a good heart. Maybe you two could actually turn out to be friends."

Wanda rolled her eyes. "Hospitable, maybe."

The ladies said goodbye. Evelyn went to do some grocery shopping. Betty Sue headed to Anna's to pick up something for her great aunt's ninetieth birthday in a few weeks. Wanda shuffled back to Sally's near the Courthouse Square to meet Todd. Her feet ached. They were not used to such abuse. Not since she had taken that church tour of Scotland four years ago.

Todd arrived at three minutes after one. It was unusual for him to be late at all. "I was starting to worry."

"Sorry, Aunt Wanda. I had my head in paperwork."

She motioned for him to have a seat. "A lot of stuff to report from last night?"

"Yeah. Murders require so many forms, statements, reports. Chief has me compiling it for the county sheriff's department."

"Why?" She hoped the chief hadn't been picking on him because of her.

He shrugged. "Jim Bob is on duty so that leaves me."

"Oh, I see. Have you identified the victim?"

Todd focused on her face with a scowl. "Why all the questions? And exactly what were you doing seeing Carl this morning?"

"Todd, I know you think I'm snooping. But I felt so guilty. If I had not organized that meeting on neighborhood watches, Carl wouldn't have gotten it in his head to go vigilante on us."

His mouth drooped as his gaze softened. "Aunt Wanda, how were you to know?"

"You could have told me he had been prowling around town for the past several nights trying to protect the cars on his lot. Surely you saw him on your patrol."

"I did, and warned him to go home. Twice. I never expected him to walk as far as the Ferguson place, though. Or shoot a guy he thinks he saw in the woods."

Wanda pulled out the mug shot. "This guy?"

"Where did you get that?" Todd snatched it, his gaze sharp as steel blades again.

"Internet." She pointed to the face. "Butch McClain. Out on parole after being arrested for a burglary in Weatherford in 2002. Suspected to be one of the ones who robbed the jewelry store in Burleson. Is he who Carl shot?"

Todd rose from the table. He bent down, his forefinger pointed straight at her nose. "Butt out. I mean it."

She folded her arms over her chest, not caring that six other patrons had stopped eating to stare at them. "The

96

citizens of this town have the right to know."

"And they will. When the chief deems it necessary." His eyes swept the room as he realized six pairs of ears, and Sally's, were glued to their conversation. He returned to his chair and lowered his voice. "Wait, you plan to bring this up tomorrow night at the meeting, don't you?"

"Among other things, like the crime stats from the NIBRS for Fort Worth, Arlington, and Dallas." She dug those out as well and slid them across the bistro table for his viewing.

He scanned the report. "You have been busy."

"It's my responsibility as chairperson for the neighborhood watch for Scrub Oak."

"Oh, is that your title, now?" He let off a nervous laugh. "Maybe I should request a transfer."

"Please don't." Wanda felt her eyes become damp and hot. The last thing she wanted to do was drive her nephew away. His absence during his college and academy years had been hard enough on her. The best thing that ever happened to the shy, introverted teen, but it had been such a lonely time for her.

Still, she felt her heart swell with pride as she took him in with her eyes. He had returned a confident, good-looking man, shoulders back, spine straight. Handsome in his uniform. Quite a catch if she did say so herself. Maybe some nice girl would notice . . .

"Aunt Wanda?" His voice echoed in her ear as if in a tunnel. She blinked back to the present.

"Todd, I want to oversee the watch teams for one reason. You. I want to make sure you are privy to whatever we might see or hear. That way you can follow up and report to the chief. Prove to him and this town you are valuable."

He chewed the side of his mouth. "And what about Jim Bob?"

"He's day shift. You know most crime happens at night."

He smiled. "Not so much anymore since more and more wives and husbands commute to the cities for work. Cleburne is just up the road. When the toll parkway extension opens, most can be in Fort Worth within a half hour tops. That'll leave houses vacant for eight to ten hours during the day."

"True. So, we should organize both day and night watches then?"

"Might be wise. Since you sweet-talked the mayor into the idea, why not? Get the whole town involved."

What did that comment mean? Did he disapprove of her efforts?

He rose from the table. "See you later."

"Wait, Todd. We haven't ordered."

"Sorry. Gonna grab a sandwich from the firehouse. They always have leftovers." He brushed her cheek with an air kiss, slapped a five dollar bill on the table, and left.

Wanda sighed and rested her chin on her hand. That had not gone as planned at all. A wall still existed between them. One she did not know how to crack, much less knock down.

She had to find a way to prove to him she had his, and the town's, best interests at heart. Thing is, she could sure use his keen perspective to help prove Carl was not a cold-blooded murderer.

If only Todd would take her word for it.

Word. Wanda shut her eyes in frustration. Of all things. She hadn't even asked him about the Scrabble letters.

Wanda spent the rest of the afternoon preparing for the meeting. Evelyn came over and helped her sort and staple together the information she'd glean into packets for everyone.

Betty Sue arrived at six with a summer salad of spinach leaves, strawberries, candied walnuts, and avocado chunks, spritzed with an apple cider and avocado oil dressing. She also brought fresh blueberry muffins with organic unsalted butter.

"It's too hot for a cooked meal." She set the bowl and muffins onto Wanda's kitchen table.

"Perfect. My stomach couldn't handle anything heavy right now anyway." She clasped her hand over her waist.

"Nervous over the meeting, Wanda? That is not like you." Betty Sue's peaches and cream face crinkled in concern.

"She and Todd had a row this afternoon in the middle of Sally's. It's all over town." Evelyn began to peel the paper away from one of the muffins.

"Not a row." Wanda set salad bowls and butter plates on the table. "Per se."

"What about?" Betty Sue eased into one of the chairs.

"I don't think Todd likes the idea of a neighborhood watch. He sees it as an excuse for me—and you two—to snoop around town, stir things up, and muddle this investigation."

"Well, it is the first murder in over twenty-something years." Evelyn rose to grab the butter from the counter.

Betty Sue raised a finger. "Unless Carl killed Aurora's husband as well. Didn't he have a crush on her in high school?"

"Who didn't have a crush on her?" Wanda faked a gag. "Anyway, I think that was his brother, Clyde or Cole or something."

Evelyn lathered on two pats of butter with gusto. "It doesn't matter who did or didn't. That would have been decades ago. Besides, we don't know that her husband's shooting was on purpose. Nor could we prove it."

"Maybe we can." Wanda sat down and gazed into the eyes of her two friends. "Forensics. We need to find out what caliber of bullet that killed Robert. Was it a shot gun or rifle?"

Evelyn sighed. "Wanda, shot guns are for dove and quail hunting. Rifles are for deer."

"Oh." She scrunched her mouth to the side. After a minute, a thought appeared. "Even so. Rifles have different calibers, too. Don't they?"

She rose and grabbed her phone. She did a search and smiled. "Look. The different brands of bullets have different calibers. Remington, Winchester, Creedmore." She scrolled across the pictures. "Tons of them. If the one that killed Robert matched the one that killed the burglar in the woods, odds would be pretty strong they came from the same gun."

"Forensics could determine that. Barrels leave marks as the cartridges leave the chamber." Evelyn shrugged. "I know because I watch CSI shows."

"We know," Betty Sue and Wanda responded together.

"Wait." Betty Sue waved her hands in front of her. "I thought you wanted to prove Carl innocent of both crimes."

Wanda nodded. "I do. I have this niggling in my brain telling me Carl didn't shoot anyone. What if someone else shot the burglar?"

"What?" Her friends responded in unison.

"Carl has rubbed a few feathers the wrong way in this community. Including the police chief's. What if someone set him up?"

Betty Sue's curls bounced as she shook her head. "No. No police corruption in our town. Never. Shame on you, Wanda Lee Warner. Think of Todd."

Wanda recognized the well-used schoolteacher scolding tone in her friend's voice. "Yeah, that is a stretch, isn't it?"

Evelyn gave off a small snort. "Set ups only occur in mystery novels, not real life. I read that somewhere."

"You're probably right." Wanda shrunk in her chair as if she sat back in first grade after being caught shooting spit wads. The only time she ever went to the principal's office. She learned that day to be sneakier to avoid getting in trouble. Had the murderer as well?

Then she felt a piercing in her chest. Sneakiness was not the way of the Cross. The truth set people free according to the Good Book.

That was what she had to discover. The truth.

Chapter Twelve

The fellowship hall hummed with conversation as people grabbed snacks, a cup of coffee, or a glass of lemonade. Wanda tapped the microphone as she stood on tiptoes to reach it. Pastor Bob trotted over to lower the pole to her height.

"I should have let you borrow the wireless."

She covered the mic with her hand. "It's fine." Then she raised her voice. "Ladies. Gentlemen. Please find your seats."

A rustling accompanied by mumbles ensued as various-sized bodies claimed chairs. Wanda did a headcount—115 people. Wow. Word had gotten around since Saturday's powwow at the Coffee Bean. Well that, and the fact there had been a shooting in town probably stirred interest.

Then she noticed the mayor, dressed in a suit, tie, and freshly ironed, starch-white shirt, take a front row seat. She probably should acknowledge him.

She motioned to Betty Sue and Evelyn to hand out the

pamphlets. "One per household, please. We only printed fifty. Sorry."

Smiles and nods let her know all was fine.

She took a deep breath. "Pastor Bob, will you start us off with a prayer?"

Heads bowed and hands clasped. After he finished, and all responded with an "Amen," Wanda began.

"I know the incident over the weekend has caused great concern. As it should. Strangers were lurking in our relatively crime-free community."

She paused when she noticed Todd and Jim Bob slip through the door and stand at the rear of the room. Chief Brooks had obviously decided not to join them. Maybe he'd sent them and stayed behind to mind the store, so to speak.

"I want to thank our mayor for attending tonight . . ." She waited as he half rose from his chair and waved to the room. "As well as two of our fine law enforcement officers." Wanda extended her hand to the back of the room and smiled her sweetest little-old-lady smile. "We are all proud of the work they do to keep us safe." Her eyes fixated onto Todd's.

Applause rippled through the crowd, growing in crescendo. A few people rose from their seats, and soon almost everyone stood, including the mayor.

Todd's cheeks grew red, and Jim Bob shuffled his feet as they both motioned a thank you for the acknowledgment.

Wanda let the din die down and then cleared her throat. "We are not here to try Carl Smithers. But it is noteworthy that he had been suspicious about the possibility of one of his cars being stolen. He told me and the police, that he had seen a shadowy figure lurking around the lot late one night. He happened to return to the office because he left his cell phone on the desk."

Whispered comments floated through the hall.

"So even before Saturday night, the possibility of crime oozing into our community existed. Which is why I included the report on the second page of your pamphlet. It is from the National Incident Based Reporting System, or NIBRS. Todd, perhaps you can explain this better than I can." She beckoned him forward.

Instead, he stayed at the back and raised his voice so the room could hear him. "The NIBRS is a division of the FBI. It has been around for twenty years, and reporting has been voluntary, but there is a new law that states all law enforcement offices in the US must begin reporting to them this year. It monitors the types of activities, both misdemeanor and criminal, that goes on in each city and state. Mrs. Warner has given you a chart of the percentage rates in North Texas over the past three years. You can see that while crime is overall down in the state, it is on the rise here, especially in the Dallas area."

The mayor stood and cleared his throat. "My office has been monitoring the NIBRS stats for several years, which is why I wholly endorse the formation a neighborhood watch force in Scrub Oak."

The mayor was definitely in campaigning mode, even

though he had gone undefeated in the last three elections. Wanda swallowed down the desire to comment as people mumbled amongst each other.

Evelyn whistled through her teeth for everyone to return their attention to the stage then nodded for Wanda to continue.

"Um, thank you, Officer Martin, and also Mayor Porter." She shifted her weight to her left foot. "Officer Martin and I met earlier today . . ." she noticed a few eyebrows cock. "He told me there is a growing trend in crime occurring during the day since more and more households have dual incomes. That means, the parents are at work, and the kids are in school, so houses are empty during normal business hours. He agrees that a watch during the day and the evening would be a good idea."

Todd opened his mouth to speak, but she cut him off. "He and Jim Bob cannot be everywhere at once. It is up to us to help them out. It is our community, too."

Several people verbalized their agreement. Applause ensued.

Wanda pumped her hands to settle the room down. "However, it is not up to us to take the law into our own hands. Only to inform and then let the police force, who is well-trained, handle things. The unfortunate incident this past weekend is exactly what should not ever happen again."

She glanced up at Todd who gave her a small head bob. Did the wall between them fissure a bit? She hoped so.

"Officer McIntyre suggested that in a town our size, we form four teams of four people each. If we are to have two shifts, then we need to double that, agreed?"

Ray O'Malley raised his hand. "I propose the women take the days and the men take the nights. Not being sexist, but, well. It seems the wise thing to do."

Jim Bob raised his hand, and Wanda acknowledged him. "During the day, one on patrol per segment would be fine. But in the evening, if a lady wants to patrol, she should have a male partner. I believe that is a well-established pattern with these types of organizations."

Wanda verbally approved. "I want to assist but I must also realize I am a senior citizen. Yes, I have more time on my hands, but I also must be prudent. We all should."

Tom Jacobs, owner of Tom's Thrift Shop and local editor of the *Oakmont County Weekly Gazette* spoke up. "What exactly are our duties?"

"Good question, Tom. The first page explains that in more detail. Everyone in town should know who is on the neighborhood watch in their area. On the back is a somewhat crude map of Scrub Oak—sorry. Art is not my forte. But it shows by color the four areas of town Officer McIntyre propose we arrange into watch groups. Therefore, we'll need at least eight people from each area to sign up to be on the teams. You will find sign-up sheets in the back on the tables, color coordinated to the map."

Several heads swiveled to locate the table.

"Once the groups are organized, each will meet to elect

a captain. Those captains and I will meet on a biweekly basis. That is, if you all agree I should be the chairperson this year."

Nods, claps, and a few whistles answered her. She noticed a proud smile creep into Todd's face, and his reaction enveloped her heart and gave her encouragement.

"Each of the thirty-two volunteers will be trained. Officer McIntyre will come down himself or send someone else to do that. I will arrange it soon. If you have any further questions, contact me, and I will find the answers."

People began to shuffle as they gathered their belongings to leave. She spoke louder to recapture their attention. "Remember, every adult over 16 in town is involved. We all need to be aware of our surroundings. We need to look out for each other and check on each other, especially those of us who are older and live alone. Scrub Oak is a fine community of caring people. Let's prove it to the rest of the North Texas area."

She stepped back from the mic and the room exploded in applause. She never expected such approval. Her stance wobbled a bit as she regained her bearings. Her heart fluttered as she fought back tears.

It felt good to be honored by her fellow citizens after the rumors over the past year. Even Mr. Baker gave her a wink. Aurora Stewart, of course, was no were to be seen. Probably in Dallas shopping at Neiman's or getting her claws gelled.

Todd weaved his way to the front and held out a hand

to escort her down the stage steps. His grip felt warm and strong. She took it gladly.

"Well done, Aunt Wanda. Look at the line forming at the sign-up table."

The mayor hovered nearby to shake hands. She chuckled. Once a politician . . .

She smiled back at Todd. "I hope you know we are doing this to help y'all and not to overstep your authority."

"Jim Bob and I both do. Now." He hooked her arm through his elbow and led her over to where Betty Sue and Evelyn stood. He addressed them all. "Ladies. Put your concentrated effort into getting this off the ground. Leave the investigative police work to us. Got it?"

Betty Sue pressed her hand to her blouse. "Of course, Todd."

Evelyn answered with a brief head bob.

Wanda swallowed. "Todd, my main efforts are to establish a viable and well-run watch. After all, there have been two deadly shootings in this town in the past year, both by a rifle. Before these happened, there had not been any killings in Scrub Oak in decades. That fact disturbs me." She took a step forward and zeroed in on his face. "Not to interfere in your business or anything, but I gather you are investigating the possibility of the two being related."

He opened his mouth, then shut it again.

Wanda turned from him and went to greet the folks who had already signed up.

Julie B Cosgrove

CHAPTER THIRTEEN

Enough people signed up to not only fully form four morning and four evening teams, but for each lady to have a partner if she chose the evening shift. Thirty-seven in all. Wanda barely slept Tuesday night due the excitement and also the responsibility she now carried. Her mind whirled like a CD in play mode.

By sunrise, she'd composed announcements and articles in her head to help get the word out. After a few phone calls, Wanda got the *Oakmont County Weekly Gazette* to agree to run an article on citizen responsibility to report suspicious activities. She spoke with the pastors at both churches about putting announcements in their upcoming Sunday bulletins.

Wanda spent the rest of Wednesday contacting each person who'd signed up, thanking them, and reminding them to attend the mandatory training on Saturday. By dinnertime, her brain had drained. Her mouth ached from talking and smiling over the phone, and she didn't have the energy to clear her kitchen table of all the paperwork.

Instead, she made a turkey sandwich and put her feet up to watch some mindless TV game shows.

And fell asleep . . .

The next morning there was a tap on her back door.

"Aunt Wanda?"

She jerked awake. What was Todd doing here in the middle of the night? Oh, her eyes blinked as the sunrays blasted through the venetian blind slats.

Not night. Morning.

She stretched and yawned. "In here." She ran her hand over her hair to smooth it a bit as she squinted to read the mantle clock. Ten after nine?

"Are you all right?" He stopped in the doorway that separated her kitchen from her dining room/living room.

She waved his concern away. "Yes, yes. Just exhausted. All this organizing has taken the stuffing out of me." She rose and padded toward the coffee pot, as Todd wisely stepped aside.

"So, I see." He pointed to her kitchen table.

"Yes." She diverted her attention from the kitchen counter and began shuffling and stacking papers.

"Here, let me make the coffee." His reply held a chuckle. "Are you up for finishing that Scrabble game?"

Scrabble? Today was Thursday. He'd shown up as if no harsh tones had occurred between them.

"Are you?"

He filled the tank with water and began doling out teaspoons of grounds into the filter. "I've been thinking

112

about the words we have been forming."

"Oh?"

"Did you preserve the game? Where is the board?"

She pointed to the top of the fridge as she moved the last of the paper stacks to her satchel.

Todd gingerly reached up and brought it down, then lifted off the dish towel. He sat, head resting in his left palm and studied the board.

"Well?" She hovered behind him, her hands on her hips. "What do you think?"

He sat back and sighed. "I'm not sure. I mean it is weird, but perhaps it's nothing more than a coincidence. 'Shot' I get. But what about the last words of cave, auto, bushes? Not only that but zero, reduce, candy, panel, and under . . . what would they have to do with anything?"

"I am not saying every word is a clue." She slid into the chair across from him, a cup of freshly brewed coffee in her hand. One sip and the cobwebs already whisked away as if a spring breeze had swished through an abandoned attic. *Thank you, Lord, for making caffeine.*

He frowned. "Then how would we determine which ones were? As if they were placed in our heads by some divine intervention, that is. Nah, I don't think so." He got up to pour himself a cup. "Got anything to eat?"

"Of course. There is some banana nut bread in the freezer. Take out as many slices as you want and nuke them."

He jerked the door open and a swirl of frigid air hit the

back of her neck. Now she really was awake.

"You want any, Aunt Wanda?"

"Sure. Two."

The words they'd played stared back at her. Perhaps he was right. She searched for clues where none existed. Even so, a tickle in the back of her mind wouldn't concede to that possibility.

He brought over the plate and the newly-awaken aroma of the bread sifted through her nose into her stomach, making it growl.

Todd snickered. "Did you even eat yesterday?"

"I'm an old woman but my brain is still intact, thank you very much. Of course, I did."

"Whoa, don't get huffy."

The angst melted like the pats of butter he spread over the slices. She took a bite and savored the taste. For a few minutes silence existed between them.

Then she bolted. Sophie. Where was Sophie? She had not wakened Wanda up to feed her. A wave of fret flowed from her head to her stomach.

"What is it? You suddenly paled."

"Where is Sophie?"

Todd's expression became contrite. "Oh, I forgot to tell you. She was last seen rooting for a bone or something else she'd buried. I am afraid your vincas were planted on top."

"Poor thing. She must be starved." She rose and whistled for her pet, who came lopping across the backyard. Her newly-planted spring flowers lay like downed bowling pins every which way along the back fence.

She poured a bowl of kibbles and petted her dachshund, cooing remorseful words. The pooch gobbled down a half cup in no time, lapped some water, and went to settle in her basket near the fridge.

Wanda blinked back tears. "How could I be so careless?"

Todd grabbed her hand. "It happens, Aunt Wanda. She is no less the wear and tear. She has a doggie door, after all. But I did worry when I saw her, and then your kitchen table."

She swiped under her eyes. "Is that why you are being nice today?"

He laid his other hand on top of hers. "I love you, Aunt Wanda. Even if sometimes you do meddle. And if you are worried that you might be losing it, I can assure you that you're not. In fact, I owe you and your sharp mind."

"You do?"

He leaned over the word play board, jostling a few of the letters from their squares. She pretended not to notice and resisted the urge to scoot them back in line.

"Forensics sent back the report on the bullet. It definitely was fired from Carl's rifle. And get this. I pulled the other report. So was the bullet that killed Robert Stewart. The scratch marks on the slugs match almost to a T."

"Carl shot them both?"

Todd's jaw stiffened. "It appears so, though he denies

it, of course."

The banana bread bounced back into her esophagus. Betty Sue had been correct.

How could that be? She'd been so sure of his innocence when she peered into his eyes on Monday.

CHAPTER FOURTEEN

Wanda told Todd she didn't feel like finishing their game. He rose, kissed her on the forehead and told her to take it easy. "You've been zipping around town at ninety-miles an hour for over a week. If you are not careful, I am going to have to arrest you for speeding."

He winked.

"Go ahead. Maybe if I am sharing a cell with Carl, I can get the truth out of him." She slumped and laced her arms over her chest.

Todd laughed. "Not sure the chief would allow it. We do have three cells, you know."

He grabbed another piece of bread and waved goodbye as he shoved it in his mouth.

Wanda stared at the back door for a few minutes as her mind tried to make sense of what Todd had revealed. Trouble was, it made no sense. Not at all. She needed to talk to Carl some more. But how?

Wait. She snapped her fingers. He must have an attorney. She could talk to him or her. Did Carl have any next of kin? Would they lend some clarity to this?

Her numbers tapped over her phone keys. In two rings, Betty Sue answered.

"Betty Sue. Do you have a minute? My memory is fuzzy. Who is Carl Smither's next of kin?"

"Well, that is hard to say. He was adopted if I recall correctly. The Arthur family took him in when his parents were killed in a car accident. He was in first grade at the time. And I think he had an older brother, too. Yes, about five or six years older. That seems right."

"Adam Arthur's parents? The fire chief?"

"Yes. They were good friends of the Smithers. In fact, Adam's dad was Carl's godfather, I think. I recall it because the car wreck happened in my third year of teaching here, in 1981. In my mid-twenties and newly married, I had never dealt with tragedy amongst students before."

"What was his brother's name? He doesn't live around here now."

"I don't recall. I do remember he was sent off to military school in San Antonio within a year or so. Ran away maybe? Let me look back in my yearbooks. I'll let you know."

Wanda thanked her and hung up. She needed to speak with Chief Arthur. Dollars to donuts, he'd arranged for an attorney to represent his step-brother.

With a plan formulating, Wanda swallowed down the last of her now cold coffee and dashed down the hall for a quick shower.

W₄

Thirty minutes later, Wanda strolled into the firehouse. She'd driven this time and parked on the street. All seemed quiet. But of course. The day neared noon. Tiptoeing past the massive red truck, she saw a door with a frosted glass panel in it and heard voices inside. The fire chief and a few of the volunteers who liked to hang out there were probably eating in the kitchen.

Wanda decided to come back in half an hour, allowing them time to eat and chat in peace.

She crossed the street to the library. Barbara waved to her. "Need a new book?"

"I'm actually looking to do some research." Wanda didn't want to share too much.

"I can help you with that." Barbara showed her how to access the information from the cloud. "I still don't understand where this mystical cloud thing is, but it seems to always retain what folks need. If you need me to print anything, just let me know."

Wanda thanked her and then scanned the old *Gazette* articles about the Smithers' accident in 1981, so she could refresh her memory.

Then she read about Robert Stewart's death last fall. The shooting happened while she had visited an old college friend in Plano, so she'd not been around to get the blow-by-blow gossip.

Wanda scrolled through six articles, three from the *Gazette*, one from the *Cleburne Times-Review,* and two from the Fort Worth *Star Telegram*, where Robert Stewart's brokerage firm had officed. One of those was the obituary.

She queued it to print out all six, though she didn't quite know how knowing the Stewart family tree would serve any purpose. Still, in all the crime shows they dig deep to discover connections. Who knew what might come of it?

The soft footsteps of a woman sounded behind her. Too petite to be Barbara's rubber-soled loafers. She peeked into the monitor to view Betty Sue's reflection.

Her best friend scooted next to her. "I saw your car parked on the street by the firehouse, but they had not seen you."

"I didn't want to disturb their lunch. How'd ya know where to find me?"

Betty Sue grinned. "Wanda, I know you. Whatcha got?"

Wanda showed her the articles. "I haven't combed through them all yet."

"Here, I thought you might want this." She pulled a yearbook from her satchel and opened it to the sticky note she'd placed as a temporary bookmark.

The school district was small enough to contain grades K-8 in one book. The first marked page of the 1981 volume showed a younger Betty Sue and then the mugshots of each of her eleven students in first grade. One, with freckles and a wild blonde crew cut sticking out in all directions, caught her eye. Carl. How innocent and unpretentious he appeared.

"This was taken two months before his parents died." Betty Sue pouted. "And, here is his brother. Sixth grade." She flipped over several pages to the next sticky note.

A boy of twelve or so gazed back. Colton Smithers. The family resemblance was strong. But this boy's eyes held a mischief. Almost maliciousness. And his life had not yet been overturned by tragedy at the time the photo had been snapped. No wonder the Arthurs had farmed him out to military school.

Betty Sue tapped it with her forefinger. "Mrs. Tucker taught him . . . or tried to."

"Priscilla's mother?"

"Uh-huh. She is in a nursing home in Keene now. But Priscilla says her memory is good much of the time. Want to go visit her tomorrow? We could take her some carnations from Kay's Flowers."

"That would be great. Thank you." She side-hugged her friend.

"Okay. Pick you up at ten." Betty Sue rose with the grace she always portrayed. She made Wanda feel like a klutz. But they were too good of friends for Wanda to concede to a twinge of jealousy.

Wanda paid Barbara for the copies and the computer use then folded up her articles and placed them in her bag. She'd pour over them later. After shoveling down a quick chicken salad at Sally's, she headed back to the firehouse at ten after one.

Just in time for the sirens to blare in her ears.

Wanda gasped and jumped to the curb as the big red machine darted out of its cave and down the street.

What on earth? The last fire in Scrub Oak was four years ago when Hazel forgot to watch a twig pile she decided to burn. She'd read that ashes were good to put around rose bushes.

Chapter Fifteen

The fire engine zipped down Main Street and turned to head up 8th. Hazel lived on 8th, but so did a lot of other people. Wanda listened for the siren to wind down, but it kept on going.

She dashed to her car, started the ignition, and took 7th to Cedar and then over to 8th. Along the way, several residents had come out of their homes and stood in their front yards gazing up the street. The warrooo-roo of the fire truck still blared. Where were they headed? Maybe to the Woodway Resort?

Then the echoing noise stopped. Wanda inched up 8th past West Elm as about ten people began to walk quickly up the street. She noticed the reflections of red lights through the trees that began the woods. The Ferguson property. Not the house, but off to the side of it, near to the entrance where the body of the burglar had been wheeled out.

The commotion had alerted Hazel who stretched up on her tiptoes and lifted her chin to get a better view. Wanda pulled over to the curb and got out. "What is going on? Do you know?"

Hazel wrapped her sweater tighter around her chest. "I have no idea. I heard the sirens and dashed from my recliner. At first, I thought they were headed for my house, then I recalled I had not been burning anything this time around." Her smile turned sheepish.

The couple next door walked over. The man motioned to the tree line. "Looks like a vagrant didn't put out his campfire."

"What vagrant?" Wanda turned to face him.

"The wife and I done seen them a couple of times over the past week."

"Them?" Wanda and Hazel responded in unison.

"Yep. A tall scrawny one, I'd say middle-aged, wouldn't you, Mabel?"

The wife nodded.

"Then another one. Gruffer looking. Figure they must be friends. At first, I thought they was on a campout. But they's been there all week, maybe more. Right, Mabel?"

She nodded again.

Wanda narrowed her eyes. Could they be the dead man's partners? The jewel thieves. "Did you tell the police?" If Todd knew and hadn't told her . . .

"Nah, wasn't any need. They seemed to keep to themselves and wasn't playing no loud music or whoopin' and hollerin' or nothing."

"Did you see them before the shooting last weekend?"

He removed his hat and scratched his balding head.

"Can't likely recall. Maybe. Didn't really connect the two."

Really? She gazed at him and then at Hazel who widened her eyes and shrugged.

Another siren's moan could be heard in the distance, the noise growing louder. All four craned their necks to the right and peered up the street.

A fire engine from Cleburne, which must have barreled down Woodway Drive from the highway, entered on 8th from the north. Jim Bob's cruiser soon followed. Both turned into the Ferguson drive and bounced over the curb onto the grass, headed for the edge of the woods.

"Ain't gonna be much grass left if they's keep doing dat." He spat to the ground. "Old Mr. Ferguson loved those lawns. Bet he's turnin' over in his grave about now."

Wanda sighed in agreement. She remembered how the Fergusons would host lawn parties in the spring, inviting anyone who wanted to come to view their flower beds. In the fall, they hosted a Halloween carnival for the kids, complete with bobbing for apples and popcorn balls and a romp through the maze. But get caught on their property at any other time, and phew. Before any child skedaddled back home, the parents, police, and pastor would have already been informed.

The foursome watched in silence. A few more neighbors wandered over, forming a small group of onlookers. Wanda excused herself and edged over to meet Tom Jacobs, the local editor of the *Oakmont County Weekly Gazette* as well as the thrift shop owner.

"Tom, know what's going on?"

He sucked in a long breath. "Picked it up on the county sheriff's broadband. Seems to be a fire in the woods. That's about all I know."

Many things can cause fires. An unattended campfire. A tossed cigarette. A piece of glass reflecting the sun's rays onto dead leaves. The usual spring rains had been delayed this year. Couple with the unseasonably warm weather, the ground already showed signs of drought. Wanda had already watered her grass twice, something she normally didn't do until early June.

Then again, Old Mr. Edwards had seen two men amongst the trees. And there had been three jewelry robbers. Did that prove the body in the morgue had been one of them? Did Butch McClain lie there or did he still wander the woods?

Todd had not been forthright in answering her about the identity of the body. How could she find out? Sneaking into the morgue for a peek seemed impractical. Todd would really be angry if she got caught. He might even arrest her.

Wait, another way tapped on her brain. If Old Mr. Edwards recognized Butch McLain as one he'd seen trespassing in the past week then it would mean someone else lay cold on the slab. And a potentially dangerous ex-con wandered around the edge of town.

She rushed to her car, retained the articles she had accumulated from her internet searches, and scurried back to Mr. Edwards. "Can you describe the older man you saw in the woods lately? Did he look like this?"

He eyed the grainy photo while Wanda's quick movements made her lungs rebel a bit. "Honestly can't say. Never got a good look at his face. Looks mean, though don't he?"

She took in a deep inhale. "I think you should tell the police. And as the newly formed neighborhood-watch chairperson, I will spread the word to keep an eye out for those two. They may be up to no good."

Mr. Edwards handed her back the photo with a scowl. "Not necessarily. Ain't the first time."

Wanda's heart leapt. "What do you mean?"

"See folks off and on over there ever since the old mansion's been deserted. Like right before that rich lady's husband got shot deer hunting. Ain't that so, Mabel?"

His wife's head bobbed once more.

"And you told no one?" Wanda tried to keep her voice steady.

"We's don't like to stick our noses where they don't belong. We keep ourselves to ourselves."

Wanda's knees buckled. How many others in her small town felt the same way? Who knew what had been going on undetected?

Well, it was high time she stuck her nose in. No matter what Todd or Aurora may think. Now that her reputation had been redeemed in the community, she considered it her civic duty to find out the reason for the connection between Robert's death and that of the stranger last week. Especially given the ballistic evidence.

Wouldn't Pete's lawn service have noticed anything unusual? Perhaps not. Once their lawnmowers revved up, the squatters would've hightailed it deeper into the woods.

Then a thought slammed into her forehead. Had Aurora's resentment to her snooping around her property on the other edge of the woods last fall been a ruse to keep Wanda from discovering her plans to have her hubby killed "by accident"?

If so, how was Carl involved? Had he and Aurora plotted her husband's demise to look like an accident? Betty Sue recalled he had a crush on her in high school. Oh, dear. She hoped not.

It just didn't seem like a thing Carl would do even if he did have a reputation of being hard to deal with at times.

CHAPTER SIXTEEN

Wanda spent the rest of the afternoon trying to gather information about the fire and Carl's youth. She baked her famous butterscotch chocolate brownies and took them to the fire station.

Adam Arthur met her with a grin peeking from his bushy moustache. "I smelled those heavenly brownies from two blocks away." He held out his hands to take the pan from her arms.

"I remembered you bid the highest on them at the church bake-fest."

"For what do I owe this honor?" He opened the door to the kitchen area of the firehouse and ushered her inside.

After he set the brownies on the table, lifted the foil, and took in a long whiff, she motioned if she could sit.

"Sure, things have quieted down now. Want a cup of coffee? Just brewed it a while ago."

One whiff told her it had been recently brewed. "I'd love one, actually. Thank you."

He poured her a cup, set the sugar bowl and a pint of

half and half near her, and got down two paper napkins for the brownies. Then he grabbed a mug with a fireman's hat on it. It read "Firemen like it flaming hot."

"Do you?" Wanda motioned with her eyes toward the saying.

His cheeks almost competed with the color of the engine now parked on the slab outside. "My coffee, yes. I am not fond of flames in general." He took a sip and shrugged. "But it's part of the job."

"Like today. Quite a ruckus."

"Yes, with the dry weather, fires like that can get out of hand quickly. We were lucky to have caught it at the early stage. Less than an eighth of an acre got charred."

Fresh or not the strength of the coffee could peel paint. She stirred in two teaspoons of sugar and a generous portion of cream. "Any idea of the cause? I mean if it were kids or vandals, I will want to let the newly forming neighborhood watches know."

He shifted in his chair. "Is that why you're here? Tom Jacobs just left asking the same thing."

"Oh?" She peered over the rim of her cup.

"Well, the *Gazette* comes out tomorrow so it will be public knowledge by then. Yes, it appears to have been started from a campfire. My guess is from someone hanging out in the old cave."

"Cave?" The words on the Scrabble board back home jumped into her mind.

"Yes, an old bootleggers cave from the 1920's lies

somewhere on the property. That's how old Ferguson Senior made his fortune. Didn't you know that?"

"No. Wasn't he the first mayor of Scrub Oak?" His statue stood on the grounds of the Courthouse Square.

"True. Back then the settlers were mostly Irish. They were against the prohibition. Then the Baptist and Seven Day Adventist ranchers and farmers moved in. Drinking is frowned on by them as you know. Almost split the town wide open just as it was forming."

"Really?" How did Wanda not know that? She'd lived there most of her life. Proved that a person could learn something new no matter their age.

"Uh-huh. But Blake Ferguson, Senior, had a tongue of honey and a manner as smooth as butter on freshly baked cornbread. He donated a huge sum of money to build First Baptist and hired the first pastor, all the while continuing to conduct business-as-usual as a dairy farmer delivering bottles of fresh milk, among other things, if you get my drift."

"Wow. I had no idea. How come my parents never told me? Or the kids in school."

The chief took a bite of brownie and chewed on it while making "mmmm" sounds. A few brown crumbs dotted his peppered moustache. Then he answered her question.

"Well, maybe I am telling tales on the playground. Honestly, it is a shady part of our township's history most would like to be forgotten. But I guess most towns in these parts have one."

"He, I mean Ferguson, Senior, did a lot of good, though?"

"Oh, absolutely. Became a teetotaler during the war. Established the library. Brought the first doctor here. Later, Blake, Junior, who we all called Old Mr. Ferguson, helped fund the Medical Center." The chief chuckled at the irony. "Blake, Junior's daughter married Pastor Richardson's predecessor. They are the ones who are disputing the will."

She knew that much. But the cave? Why had she never learned of it? She'd lived here most of her life. In fact, the word had not hit Betty Sue's radar either. And she was born here.

"How many people know about this cave?"

Adam Arthur leaned back in his chair. "Not too many I suppose. Most who did are probably pushing up daisies in the cemetery. I discovered it when my brothers and I stumbled upon it."

"Carl and Colton?"

"That's right. Half-brothers really. Colton supposedly went there with his buddies to smoke cigarettes behind my parents' back when we lived at the brick Federalist-style home on 7th and West Elm. The Kings live there now, you know."

"I understand Colton was pretty wild."

The chief stared at the ceiling. "Yea, that's true. He possessed an anger deep down inside that gnawed at him. But he had a bad-boy charm about him. All the girls were drawn to him like dieters to chocolate." He lifted the remainder of his brownie, popped it in his mouth, and winked.

"But not Carl, right? He always seemed shy to me."

"Carl remained the quiet one, believe it or not. Funny how two kids turn out so different. Especially after my parents shoved his brother into military school. Carl didn't come out of his shell until after college. Sometimes, kids find themselves once they leave home. Some, of course, don't. He did. Returned a confident man destined to make a name for himself." The chief picked at his thumb nail. "Didn't think it would be this way, though."

Wanda leaned in. "I don't think he did it. A little voice inside of me keeps saying Carl is not the one."

The chief scoffed. "That makes two of us. Perhaps the only two." He drained his mug and stood. "Getting a lawyer friend of mine from Dallas to represent him. He knew Carl at college as well. In the same fraternity."

"Good. He needs someone on his side. I went to see him."

"I know. He told me. You want to help prove his innocence, don't you?"

"Yes."

"Mind if I ask why? I know Carl has ruffled a few feathers the wrong way around here over the years. But to tell the truth, car salesmen are often that way."

She rose from the table and lifted her purse onto her shoulder. "I can't place a finger on it, Chief. It is just a gut instinct."

He laid a hand on her arm. "It may be enough for you but a jury will need more. Anything I can do to help, you let me know."

"I will." She turned to leave.

Adam Arthur held the door open for her. "Thanks for the brownies. Oh, and Wanda?"

"Yes?"

"Stay away from that cave if you find it."

She flashed him a quick smile. How did he know she wanted to seek it out?

CHAPTER SEVENTEEN

That evening she worked at her computer until her eyes saw spots. She read all she could about the town's history, the Fergusons, and the Arthurs. The two families settled soon after the First World War. Blake Ferguson, Senior, and Adam's father had been war buddies, and the idea of peace and quiet in the rural area of North Texas fit the bill. They bought some dairy cows and land along where Woodway Resort stood now, across the lake from the mansion. Adam's father soon decided dairying was not his forte, so he instead opened the first general store in town. Both did well.

Situated near the railroad that ran from Galveston to Fort Worth's stockyards, the town had thrived in those years. Wanda wondered if perhaps Adam had not been entirely truthful, though. Had his dad and Ferguson, Senior, been in business together in other ways after the war? Is that how he knew about the cave?

About nine, her vision began to blur through her yawns. She whistled for Sophie to come in from the backyard and

135

remembered her scattered vincas. All dead now probably after being uprooted so viciously and then lying in the heat all day. Oh, well. She had other issues to handle besides planting flowers.

After a wonderfully soothing hot shower, she crawled under her covers and didn't stir the rest of the night, not even for a night trip to the bathroom.

The next morning, Betty Sue rapped on her back door at 9:42 a.m., dressed in a summer frock of tiny pastel flowers. Wanda felt frumpy in her navy, pleated skirt and white blouse but smiled. "Have a thermos of cinnamon vanilla latte, with stevia, for the road."

"Yum. Let's head out. Autumn Villas is about a thirty minute drive. I looked it up. It is northwest of Keene heading toward Joshua. It's run by the Adventists. I figure we may as well scope it out. One day we may be roommates there."

The idea had never occurred to Wanda. "Let's not rush it. We are only in our sixties."

Her friend's laugh almost qualified as a melody. "I called ahead and told them we wanted to visit with Mrs. Tucker. The lady told me the timing was perfect. Mrs. Tucker is having a very lucid day today."

Wanda silently thanked God for this small favor. She

didn't know how Colton could possibly fit into this, but perhaps the old teacher's long term memory held an answer.

She poured them each a cup of coffee. "Betty Sue. Did you know there was a cave on the Fergusson property?"

"Why, no." Betty Sue swiveled to face Wanda. Her hands on the steering wheel followed her eyes, almost swerving them into the bar ditch. After she righted the car, she wrinkled her button nose. "Wait, wasn't that one of the words on the Scrabble board?"

"Yes. I heard about it from Adam Archer. I went to ask him about Carl and also the fire."

"Oh. I saw it made the front page of the *Gazette* but hadn't read it yet."

"I did." Wanda adjusted her belt. "But Tom mentioned nothing about a cave in his article. Simply that it had been a campfire left unattended. And get this. You know that aloof old couple that lives next to Hazel? They say they have seen people camping out in the woods off and on since the mansion was vacated."

"No way. And they never said a thing?"

She scowled. "They keep themselves to themselves."

Betty Sue whistled. "Man, do we ever need that neighborhood watch then."

"I agree. But there is more." Wanda filled her in on the history of the town's beginnings, including the Ferguson enterprise.

"I had no idea. My word. I wonder if old Mrs. Tucker knows anything about how the Fergusons empire came to be."

"I do, too, Betty Sue. I do, too." Wanda peered out the side window as they pulled into the driveway leading to Autumn Villas.

The setting oozed peace and quiet. Oaks shaded manicured lawns edged with flower beds. In the middle of the drive, a fountain danced and splashed into a turquoise tiled pool with koi and water lilies. Birdsong meandered through the grounds in a natural melody of calmness.

Wanda rolled down her window. "I could do this one day."

"Um-hm." Betty Sue turned off the ignition. "Maybe we should make reservations while we're here. I understand their waiting list is long."

"Not that long, I hope. I don't plan to move in until at least 2042."

Betty Sue laughed. "From your lips to God's ears, my dear."

They strolled up the colonial stairs to the double-beveled doors. Comfortable, classic-seating groups perched on oriental rugs over marble floors. Off to the right, a lady smiled from behind a mahogany desk. In a soft voice, she asked if she could help them.

"We are here to see Mrs. Tucker. I used to teach with her." Betty Sue noticed the sign requiring them to sign in and produce a picture I.D. She dug in her wallet for her driver's license and bent to sign in.

Wanda did the same.

The lady eyed their identifications and nodded. "Very well. She is in Room 248, but this time of day you will probably find her in the sunroom playing cards. It's through the open French doors down on your right."

As they strolled in the direction the receptionist indicated, Wanda leaned closer to Betty Sue's ear. "Will you recognize her?"

"I hope so. It's been sixteen years, I think. No wait. I visited her over Christmas in . . ." She halted and looked at the ceiling as if the answer would appear on the rafters. "Hmmm, 2012. Yes, that was it. The fiftieth anniversary for the school's opening. We formed a committee to seek out all the retired teachers and present them or their heirs with a plaque. It read, *Teachers help others be reachers.* I know reachers isn't a word, but the committee voted for the phrase." She shrugged.

Wanda kept silent and followed her into the softly-lit room dotted with potted plants, tables for four, and lounge chairs. Quiet, classical music played in the background. Some of the residents dosed in wheelchairs. A group of white-haired ladies sat around one of the tables, their voices cheerful.

"Four spades."

"Five hearts."

"Now, Mildred, are you sure? You've been overbidding all day."

"I'm sure, Agnes." She lifted her chin and set down the first trump card.

"Mrs. Tucker?" Betty Sue approached the third lady in the group. "It's Betty Sue Simpson. I taught first grade when you taught sixth. Remember?"

A light behind the clouded blue eyes brightened. Then she held out shaky, blue-veined hands to Betty Sue. "My dear. How nice of you to visit. Shall we chat over there?" She pointed to a grouping of chairs by the fish tank. She put her cards on the table. "I'll be the rummy."

The other ladies nodded.

Betty Sue leant her an elbow as she wobbled to rise and grasp her cane. Once seated, she straightened her skirt over her knees, a touch of feminine modesty probably drummed into her memory by her mother decades ago.

"Now, tell me why you ladies have come to visit."

Betty Sue introduced Wanda and briefly explained what had happened that landed Carl in jail.

"Oh, dear. And he was the quiet one. Not like his brother."

Wanda inched forward in her chair, hands on her knees. "Can you tell us about the Smithers boys? I understand their parents were killed?"

"Yes, in a car accident coming back from a football game in Waco. The authorities assumed that Mr. Smithers fell asleep at the wheel and edged over the I-35 median into oncoming traffic. Didn't have barriers back then, you know. Only wildflowers and oleander, thanks to LBJ's wife. What was her name?"

"Lady Bird." Wanda smiled.

"Ah, yes. Classy lady. Anyway, the Arthurs took the boys in, even though they had two children of their own. A boy and a baby girl. Carl became even more withdrawn as I am sure you remember. Colton, well, he became a handful. Always smoking cigarettes. Sneaking out at night with Tommy Reynolds and Bubba Huffman in the eighth grade. They were a bad influence. I recall old Chief Robinson dragging them out of those woods by their ears a couple of times when they were truant." She let off a little cackle, but her eyes drooped a bit. "The poor man tried until he practically turned blue and still could not turn them around."

Wanda said each name five times in her mind to imprint them there. She made a mental note to look them up in the old school yearbooks. "What happened to them?"

She shifted her gaze to something outside the window. Her voice lowered, as if now far away in the past. "I don't recall. I know Colton was shipped off to a military academy. I think Tommy dropped out of school. Or perhaps they expelled him. He lived with his dad on the Ferguson Dairy Farm. His dad was one of the hands, hired right out of high school. They lived in one of the workers' shacks, but his father basically let the boy run wild."

"No mother?" Wanda had gotten out an advertisement for a dress shop in Cleburne she'd found in her purse and had begun to scribble the information on the back of it.

"Nope. Died shortly after childbirth I believe." She continued to stare out the window as if her mind tried to grab a piece of the past. "The man tried, I guess. He worked long hours at the dairy farm and was a loyal employee. I seem to recall that Tommy got in trouble, real trouble in seventh grade. Mr. Ferguson offered him a job assisting the gardener on the grounds after school in the spring and summer months. For a while, it seemed to do the trick. Then, after Colton's parents died, Tommy seemed to regress. I guess they were bad for each other. Tommy, Bubba, and Colton used to hop the trains and ride into Fort Worth. Would be gone for days. Had the police after them several times."

"And the other one? Bubba?"

The old woman slowly shook her head. "Arrested for vandalism and underage drinking when he was in tenth grade. Sent to juvenile hall. I have no idea what happened after that. Some of them you just can't turn around." She dipped her head and began to twist the old wedding band on her left hand.

Betty Sue picked up on the cue and changed the subject. "So, how are your son and his family? They live in Dallas, right?"

The lady raised her gaze, the twinkle returning. For the next several minutes they let her chat on about her grandkids, one of which had married and was expecting her second child. The other two were career-minded.

Then, Wanda could tell the woman's energy waned. She stood and extended her hand. "Thank you so much for taking the time to speak with us today, Mrs. Tucker. God bless and keep you."

"And you, my dear. What was your name again?"

"Wanda. Wanda Warner."

"Ah, I remember you. You came when you were in third or fourth grade, right? I never taught you because the year you would be in my class, I was staying home with my baby girl, but I recall you being one of the brightest students in your class. Always getting awards. Went to state in the spelling bee, didn't you?"

Wanda felt her cheeks warm. "That was a very long time ago."

After waving goodbye, Wanda mulled over the information they had gleaned as they traipsed to the car. "Do you recall those two boys, Betty Sue?"

"I do now that she mentioned them. Hoodlums. Bullies from day one."

"And Tommy's father worked on the dairy farm. I wonder if he knew about the cave?"

"I doubt it." Betty Sue clicked the fob to open the car door. "He would have been hired after high school in the late 1940's. Long after the bootlegging stopped."

Wanda waited until they were buckled in then she asked. "How do you figure that?"

"Easy. Carl was in my first grade class in 1981 so he had to have been born in 1974 or '75. Colton, in sixth grade, would have been born in 1968 or '69. So, if Tommy's dad was hired right out of high school that would have been in 1948 or '49."

"No later than 1950 to have a twelve-year-old boy."

"Right. Which means he worked there for over thirty years. The dairy farm closed in '82 during the oil crisis."

"Of course. Many Texans lost their shirts in those years. Scrub Oak almost became a ghost town. Big Bill worried that we'd have to move."

Betty Sue took her hand from the wheel to squeeze her friend's fingers. "I am so glad you didn't."

"Me, too. We both planted gardens to get by, remember? We'd trade veggies back and forth to make soups."

"I do. And pooled our dollars to buy a ham hock to share."

Wanda let off a long sigh. "Tough times. Bill would take the church bus into Fort Worth to work, along with six other men, because we couldn't afford gasoline for the car even at rock-bottom prices."

"My Henry travelled, as you know, selling farm equipment. He had to get that job on a farm in Kansas. For three years, the girls and I only saw him on holidays."

"And Bill would come by every evening to check on you."

She smiled. "I have never been more grateful for you and your husband."

Wanda felt the heat rise from her neck into her eyes. She hated sentimentality. Once she started crying there was no stopping the dam from bursting for at least a half hour. She always preferred to let that happen late at night when she lay in her own bed. She swallowed and redirected the conversation. "I imagine the Fergusons had invested heavily in oil and mineral rights back then."

"Yes. And as you recall, the wells around here all shut down."

Wanda snapped around in her seat, straining the belt against her shoulder. "That's right. There are two still abandoned ones just a few miles north of town. Big and Little Betsy."

"Uh-huh. I used to trek my students there to look at them. They're fenced off now to preserve them from vandals, but there's a historical marker plaque that describes their heyday."

"I bet the kids had fun."

"Yes. The rigs were on the edge of the old dairy farm. Betsy is often a nickname for a cow. Get it? The Fergusons sold most of the land in the eighties to that investor who tore down the worker's shanties and established the resort."

Wanda felt a shudder ripple up her spine. "Wasn't his name Otto Ford?"

"And everyone kiddingly called him 'Auto' behind his back because he was always sputtering about his money and prestige. A real motor-mouth." Betty pulled over, stopped the car, and put her hands to her opened lips.

The two stared at each other and then whispered in unison. "The Scrabble board."

Julie B Cosgrove

CHAPTER EIGHTEEN

Much of what Betty Sue recalled had escaped Wanda's radar. But then, Betty Sue had been a teacher and naturally knew everything about her students and their families.

Wanda figured she must have been asleep at the wheel through many of those years. Busy raising kids and holding down the fort as her hubby commuted long hours. She'd spent most of her time figuring out how to scrape pennies together to send her two kids to state universities, though both also had held jobs and earned partial scholarships.

Then, after Bill's stroke in 2004, she became the bread winner doing freelance writing. She continued to do that for fifteen years, even after his second, fatal one hit in 2006. It kept her going until she decided to retire in 2019.

Perhaps she had become bored with the easy life and needed a project. Maybe that's why her energy had renewed since forming the watches and investigating Carl's innocence. Is that why she felt so adamant about resolving the mystery? Wanda decided not to delve too deeply into the whys for now and concentrate on the who and how.

She spent the rest of the afternoon in the library with Betty Sue, flipping through old yearbooks, scanning old newspaper articles, and reminiscing. Somehow, if the Scrabble board clues rang true, the Ferguson cave where Colton, Tommy, and Bubba used to do things they were not supposed to do, and "Auto" Ford were tied together. But how, they had yet to figure out.

"Let's look up Auto. A big shot investor has to have a paper trail in the newspapers."

"Maybe his family and the Fergusons ran in the same social circles." Betty Sue clicked at the keyboard. "Let's check out the society pages in the Dallas paper around the 1980's."

"Okay. While you are doing that, I'll scan the Wall Street Journals and financial news."

A half hour later, the two had pieced together enough information to link the two families. The Fords, distant relations to Henry's dynasty, moved from auto manufacturing and sales into real estate development. Otto's father, Aloysius had been a self-made man. He had sold the land, which became the dairy farm, to the original Ferguson patriarch. They may have been involved in the bootlegging together, but the oil discovered under the land had been the true investment. During the early1900's people began drilling for oil all over the state. Because of the large pockets discovered in the area, many young men settled here and signed up to be rough necks working the drills. Some were not paid but were promised a small percentage of the mineral rights if oil was struck. Aloysius used that money to put himself through college and law school.

When the Depression hit, Aloysius Ford became the attorney for many of the landowners and oil drillers. Recalling his own past hard times, he traded mineral rights for his services since cash was scarce. When the economic boom exploded after WWII, he cashed in on those favors and made millions. The Fergusons had been one of the families he had represented. Tied economically and socially for decades, it only made sense for Otto Ford to bail the Ferguson dynasty out and buy their land in the 1980's, since he already retained most of the mineral rights.

"Perhaps he knew the wells were drying up. So, he figured the land might be worth something."

"Reasonable to me Wanda." Betty Sue sat back and stretched her arms over her shoulders. "My eyes are tired. Let's call it a day and go grab a burger."

Wanda laughed, then duck her head when she caught Barbara's stern glare, her finger to her lips. In a low voice she bent closer to Betty Sue. "You want junk food??"

Betty Sue folded her notebook and grabbed her purse. "Occasionally." She raised her nose and exited the library.

Wanda scrambled to gather her things and followed. Disappointment set in when Betty Sue let her order first. She got a cheeseburger, onion rings and iced sweet tea. Betty Sue ordered a hamburger, no bun, a bottle of water, and a salad.

"Since when did Better Burgers start making salads?"

Betty Sue scooted into the booth with her tray. "They always have as far as I know." With a shrug she stabbed her plastic fork into a piece of lettuce.

Wanda's appetite waned. She ate half her sandwich, only three onion rings, and sipped her tea. Her mind, however, kept churning. Thoughts tumbled as if someone shuffled the tiles in a bag for a Scrabble game. Tiny bits of information, none of them making words or sense.

"So then what have we learned from our afternoon of intense research?"

Betty Sue tilted her head to the side as she sliced a piece of hamburger and dipped it in mustard. "I am not sure."

"Well, other than Otto Ford had to have known Colton, and Tommy and Bubba." Wanda crunched down on another onion ring. Heck with the grease, cholesterol, and calories. She'd bought them. Why waste them?

"How? Why would a rich tycoon have anything to do with three hoodlums?" Betty Sue chomped on more salad.

Wanda sighed. "Maybe they did odd jobs for him while the resort was being built?"

Betty Sue pushed the thought away with her hand. "I am sure he had a foreman, and contractors to oversee the day labor. And those kids were not the type to get their armpits sweaty with an honest day's work. Believe me. Although Mrs. Tucker did mention Tommy had worked on the Ferguson grounds a while."

"Well, I still feel there is some connection."

Betty Sue wiped her mouth. "Then there is only one

way to find out. Ask Carl or find Colton and ask him."

"I know." Wanda rested her chin on her hand and scooted the saltshaker next to the pepper. "Not an easy task to undertake."

Betty Sue patted her arm. "If anyone can figure this out, you can."

Wanda wish she had her friend's confidence. Trying to talk with Carl would ruffle too many feathers, especially Todd's, whose she had slowly begun to smooth over, she hoped. And how in the world could she locate Colton? Mrs. Tucker had helped with some background information, but nothing beyond the fact he'd been sent to military school decades ago.

Wait. Perhaps the school's alumni association could help. Even if he was expelled or dropped out, they might have some information. It was worth a try.

"Betty Sue. I better go. Thanks for all your help today." She snatched the ticket from the table. "Dinner is on me." She shuffled her things together and rose after leaving a nice tip on the table.

Betty Sue, stopped, her mouth opened to receive her last bite of hamburger meat. She set her fork down with a questioning frown. "Bye."

"I'll call ya later." With a wiggle of her fingers, Wanda left, then realized Betty Sue had driven. That meant she had to walk home. The bank clock read ninety-two degrees.

With a groan, she trudged up 12th Street the four blocks to Spruce. Well, maybe she'd work off that last onion ring on the way.

Dripping wet and panting, she unlocked her back door to be greeted by an overanxious dachshund bouncing and twirling like a kid on Christmas morning.

"What is it, Sophie? My word. You act as if I'd been gone for a month." She set her things down on the kitchen counter and reached in the fridge for the jug of iced water.

Sophie whimpered and plopped into her bed, her long chin draping over the edge.

Wanda laughed. "All right." She bent down to rub the velvety ears. Soft, pleading, brown eyes gazed back at her. After a minute of petting and cooing she dug a doggie bone treat from the box and gave it to her pet.

Maybe Sophie would leave her alone long enough to make a few phone calls. Back on her laptop, Wanda searched for military schools near San Antonio. She ruled out Texas Military Institute because it was coed. She doubted the Arthurs would have sent Colton to a school with girls. San Antonio Academy. All boys. Formed after WWI. Known for its disciplinary and academic excellence. Bingo.

Wanda dialed the number.

The receptionist answered on the fourth ring.

Wanda put on her best little old lady voice. "Hello, I hate to bother you but we are a bit desperate. You see there was a shooting in our North Texas town and one of the men was identified as Carl Smithers."

Wanda stopped and swallowed. Not a lie, exactly.

She'd confess that tonight in her prayers, or she'd never get to sleep.

"I am chairperson of our neighborhood watch association and we are trying to locate his next of kin."

"Oh? How could we possibly help?" A squeak of a chair spring came over the phone speaker.

"He had a brother named Colton Smithers. The boys were orphaned back in the eighties and Colton, being the eldest, was sent to your school by a benefactor. I hoped your Alumni Association might have some record of his whereabouts."

"Let me connect you with our admissions director. She has been here for over thirty years. Perhaps she might know something."

Wanda waited on hold as "I am Proud to Be an American" played. Halfway through the second verse, a voice answered and introduced himself.

"Oh, hello." Why she had expected a female voice, Wanda didn't know.

"Brenda explained your situation."

Good. She didn't want to have to repeat herself.

"Yes, unfortunately, I do recall Colton Smithers. Unruly, he spent most of his time in detention. Ran away several times, but the police always located him. He had an anger deep in his eyes I had rarely seen. And he fed it regularly. Hated school. Hated the other boys. Hated any routine." He paused and let off a sad chuckle. "Even hated the food."

"Don't most kids?"

"Yes, ma'am. About the only thing normal about him. Eventually, we had to expel him. Packed him up and sent him back to your town, I assume."

"Scrub Oak?" Mrs. Tucker surely would have mentioned that. Or Chief Arthur.

"Let me see."

Wanda heard computer keys clicking.

"Hmm, the archive records haven't all been computerized. Only back to 1990. May I call you back? I am afraid I will have to get someone to dig through the old filing cabinets in the basement. That may take a day or two."

"No problem. Any help would be appreciated."

"I am sorry to hear about his brother."

Wanda cleared her throat. "Yes. Thanks."

She disconnected the call. Sophie raised her head and cocked it. But her tail didn't wag.

With a groan, Wanda got up. "I know. I know. I confess. I twisted the truth a tad."

Sophie let of a long sigh and turned in her bed until she faced the wall.

"Fine. Now my dog is upset with me."

CHAPTER NINETEEN

Brenda at San Antonio Academy called back Friday morning. Colton Smithers had been expelled at the age of 16 in 1984. Two teachers assigned to escort him back to Scrub Oak lost track of him when they stopped for gas. After a three-day search with the help of the Waco Police, the school gave up and filed papers of truancy.

Wanda thanked her for the information and drove to the fire station to speak to Fire Chief Arthur. She found him at his desk, half-hidden behind a stack of folders. She tapped on the partially opened door.

He smiled and waved her in. "Hey, there. Bringing me more brownies?"

She suddenly felt contrite. Not for coming emptyhanded as much as trying to bribe him with sweets the first time. "No, I didn't bring y'all anything. Sorry." She fanned her face. "Too hot to bake."

"Tell me about it. Try wearing fire-retardant gear in this weather." He motioned her to sit down and shoved the files a few inches to the right so she could see him better.

"Are you too busy?"

"Nah, Wanda. Glad to have the reprieve. My eyes were starting to cross." He removed his glasses and wiped them. "Preparing for a State Audit."

"Is that bad?"

He gave her a quick shrug. "Nah, the Texas Commission of Fire Prevention drops in every few years to make sure we are compliant. Routine stuff. I admit, I haven't been diligent about keeping up with the paperwork, though. Hate doing it." He shrunk into his shoulders. "The wife handles all the bills and things at home."

"Ah."

"Coffee?"

She smiled at his hospitality. "No, thank you. I know you're swamped, so I'll get straight to the point. I learned that Colton was expelled from military school in 1984 and ran away on the way back to Scrub Oak."

He took a sip of his mug and then peered at her over the rim. "You've been busy."

"Why didn't you tell me?"

"Why do you need to know?"

Wanda took a breath. "Colton is Carl's only living kin, right? I wanted to find him and let him know about his brother."

Adam Arthur scoffed. "Colton wouldn't care. They haven't seen each other in decades. What is this really about, Wanda? What are you sticking your nose into now?"

She fiddled with the strap of her purse. "I think Otto

Ford knew Colton and he knew about the bootlegger cave. And I know that Butch McClain is suspected to be one of the robbers. There is a wanted bulletin in the police station to be on the lookout for him in connection with the Burleson robbery."

"So?"

She eased forward in the chair. "Butch must have known about the cave, too."

"How do you figure that?"

"The proximity to the crime scene. Hazel's neighbors say they have seen squatters near the edge of the woods off and on. It would make sense they are using the cave. I'm betting that Carl caught him coming out or heading in and shot him."

"This Butch fellow?" He set the coffee mug down.

Wanda nodded. The pungent aroma hit her nose. She was glad she'd refused a cup. Who knew how long ago it had been brewed?

"Thing is, how did Butch McClain find out? It had to be from Colton, Tommy or Bubba, or Otto Ford, whose family partnered in many Ferguson ventures. Unless," she narrowed her gaze. "You told him."

The chief sat back in his chair and laughed. "First of all, Butch is not the man in the morgue. That I know for a fact. I was at the scene. Second, Otto hasn't been seen around here for years. Not since Ferguson, Junior passed on."

"But Otto owns the resort."

"That's where you are wrong, Wanda. He did own it, but he sold it to Robert Stewart a few years back."

"Aurora's husband?"

"Yep."

"So, Aurora owns it now?"

"Her name is on the deed. She has a management corporation out of Dallas running it." He flipped through some of the folders in the stack and pulled out one. "Ah, according to our last inspection report in February, it is managed by C.L.S. Enterprises."

An idea bolted through Wanda's brain. "What was Colton's middle name?"

"Louis. Why?"

She grinned.

The chief closed the folder. "Uh-uh. No way Colton would be a head honcho for a development management firm. He was no good. Never had been. If you want to look for him, check the state criminal records. My guess is he's rotting in the state pen."

Wanda lifted herself gracefully from the chair. "You truly have had no contact with Colton Louis Smithers?"

He crossed his heart. "Had no reason to. The heartache he caused my daddy . . . I swear he went to his grave thinking he had disappointed his best friend by not raising the boy right. I only hope he found out the truth once he got up to the pearly gates."

"And that would be?"

"Ain't nobody's fault. That boy was born bad." He

swiped his hand over the back of his neck, no longer making eye contact. "I hated him. So did Carl. The best day of our lives was when we heard he'd bailed from his military school escorts on the way back here."

"Because?"

"Because it meant he wouldn't be back to mess us around." He stared at his knuckles, now clenched and white against the edge of his desk. Clearing his throat, he released his hands and dropped them into his lap.

Wanda swallowed. She had never seen Adam Arthur riled before. The man always exhibited calm under pressure. She nodded, whispered her thanks, and left his office.

All the way back home, negativity hung on her shoulders like a cape woven of gloom. Not that she blamed Adam for disliking Colton. The kid probably bullied him. He'd invaded Adam's homelife and disrupted it horribly.

Perhaps Colton was a dead end. Adam Arthur was right. A kid that unruly had to have been sucked into the criminal underground a long time ago. Dollars to donuts she'd find him in the state prison roster doing twenty-to-life.

CLS could stand for anything. Commercial Lending Services. Corporate Leasing Subsidiaries. Charles Lincoln Smith for all she knew.

And Otto, or Auto, was a red herring. The Scrabble words were merely coincidental. She'd been spinning in circles, wasting time and energy for nothing. And all she'd accomplished was to stir up hurt feelings and alienate her nephew. She didn't want to topple the fragile bridge she had constructed back to his good side.

She slumped back into her house and plopped down in her recliner with a huge, shaky sigh.

Sophie waddled over and laid her chin on Wanda's foot.

Warmth spread over her. "Hey, Soph." She reached to scratch the pup's head. "Guess I am nothing but an old busybody after all. When will I ever learn?"

The dog peered at her with mournful eyes, then whimpered.

She bent to scratch her ears. "At least I have you. You don't care about burglars or caves, or bodies in morgues, or even words on a silly game board, do you? As long as I feed you, you are happy."

Then it hit her.

Butch McClain was not the body in the morgue. The chief was certain because he had been there at the scene. That meant he could be hanging around Scrub Oak. The gang leader.

Wait. Then who *was* in the morgue? And why had Arthur not revealed that information to her?

CHAPTER TWENTY

She opened the back door to let Sophie out, a ritual even though her pet had a doggie door. The dog would wag her tail in fast motion and do a dip and stutter dance. Wanda would say, "Out?"' and then go to the back door and rattle the knob. The things people do for their pets.

As she watched Sophie bounce through the grass after a butterfly, she heard old Frank Paterson hacking and coughing across the back fence. His fits worried her, but he always seemed to be able-bodied otherwise, even at the age of eighty-seven. Several times since her husband passed, he had done a few things for her like fix a drawer handle, check the pilot light in her furnace, or show her how to correctly use a plunger. She had, in exchange, fixed him soups, stews, or casseroles. Neighborly stuff.

"Hey Frank. Out for your afternoon fresh air jaunt?" The man walked the perimeter of his backyard twice a day, every day, weather permitting.

"Yep." He let out another series of phlegmy coughs and then peeked over the fence top. "Wanda. Sorry I didn't make the meeting. The battery on my portable oxygen tank was too low. Can't patrol much, not with this tube thingy in my nose all the time, but I can report stuff. Especially during the day."

Frank had been neighborhood watching for at least twenty years since his wife was called home by the angels. It occupied his days, sitting at his desk, reading, and peering through the large double window. She had seen the diary in which he daily recorded the number of cars, dogs, people, and birds he'd noticed.

Wanda often felt sorry for him and had thought about hauling her Scrabble board over once a week to give him a breather . . . oh, bad choice of words. But Frank seemed content with his lifestyle. Never in a bad mood.

She walked closer to him. "That would be a good thing. I know you are diligent about keeping an eye on things in the neighborhood and we all appreciate it."

He dipped his head, the bald spot on top suddenly turning pink. "I do what I can. In fact, I saw something about an hour before the sirens sounded." He turned his head to cough then continued in a gravelly voice. "Can't rightly recall what, but you are more than welcome to come read what I jotted down."

"Okay. Be right there."

"Let yourself in the back. It's open." He waddled away, the clicks and whirs of his portable oxygen tank fading.

Wanda waited about five minutes before heading over there. She figured that was the proper thing to do. Besides, it gave her time to plate some crackers, cheese, and grapes. She slipped through his back gate and tapped on the door before entering.

"Frank?" Even though he had given up the cigars ten years ago and only sucked on pretzel sticks now, the stale odor clung to his environment like a distant memory. It reminded Wanda of her mother's bungalow. Her father had been an avid pipe user. Sometimes she'd sneak into the attic and open the old chest filled with their scrapbooks and memorabilia and whiff in the distinct aroma of the past. Almost as if they clung there in wisps of love ready to embrace her.

He sat at his desk. "Ah, there you are." He half-turned as his yellowed eyes followed her hands setting the plate of food near his reach. "A treat. How thoughtful."

A shaky hand grabbed a cracker and placed a piece of cheese on it. She waited until he had chewed it before asking to see his notebook.

"Here you are. Gaze to your heart's content. May mean something or nothing at all." He snatched another cracker.

She pulled up the wooden rocker that perched in the corner of the room and spread the spiraled pages flat.

His writing was precise, even though a bit squiggly from his hand tremor. The morning of the fire in the Ferguson woods, he had noted three cardinals in the oak tree, one brighter red and flapping its wings. A fledge?

Two squirrels in a spiral dance around the trunk then zipped into the limbs and began barking.

11:35. Priscilla Tucker walked by with her labradoodle.

Wanda thought it strange that Priscilla was not at the Coffee Bean by then. "Frank, is that normal?" She tapped her fingernail at the entry.

"Oh, yes. Everyday around that time, like clockwork. Figure that is how long it takes her to leave the Coffee Bean and get back before the lunch crowd hits. Heads for Pecan Park. Her condo only has a small patio and xeriscaping in the front. That dog of hers has a bladder problem, you know."

No, she didn't and wasn't sure she'd wanted to know. Still, she made a mental note to ask Priscilla if she noticed any unusual activity that day, though she doubted it. The fire happened a good hour or so later. She'd have been back at the Coffee Bean by then.

12:15. Strange man in flannel plaid shirt carried firewood. Seemed in a hurry.

Noticed the Buckley's side gate open.

Wanda glared at Frank.

"Uh-huh. That is what I thought, too. I think he stole some of their firewood. But why he'd do such a thing in the summer I have no idea."

"For a campfire. But surely the woods contain ample material. Twigs, leaves."

"Perhaps." Frank scratched his chin. "But that'd burn awfully fast and smoke a lot. Maybe they didn't have an ax or hatchet to chop up branches."

That's what Wanda liked about Frank. His practical knowledge. "Do you recall what he looked like? Young, old? Dark hair or light? Skinny or tall?"

"Well, let me see . . ." He leaned back in his chair and closed his eyes. "I'd say not too young. Not skinny, more muscular. Dark hair, but, wait." His eyes opened and widened. "I think he had salt and pepper hair with a bit of a scraggly beard. As if he had not shaved in a week or so."

Wanda smiled. "If I brought you a picture, do you think you could tell if it was him or not?"

"Reckon so. Maybe."

"Good. I'll be right back."

She dashed over to her house, grabbed her research folder, and headed back. She rushed inside Frank's kitchen, this time not bothering to knock, and strutted toward his den that faced the front sidewalk. He sat at the desk polishing off the snacks.

"Here." She sat back down in the rocker and leaned forward as she opened her folder. Flipping through the papers to find the grainy photo, she pointed to the mug shot of Butch McClain. "There. Is that him?"

Frank took the paper in his hand and held it up. He squinted and adjusted his glasses. Somewhere in the house a clock ticked. A sparrow chirped outside.

After a minute, which seemed more like ten, he jutted out his lower lip. "Could be at that. Couldn't swear to it in court, though. But yes, I'd say the resemblance is there."

Frank handed it back to her.

Wanda let out a long breath. She was now convinced that her suspicions were true. Butch McClain had been wandering her neighborhood. No doubt about it.

Protocol as chairperson of the neighborhood watch demanded she report it to the police.

But would they believe her? She needed more proof.

She walked across to the Buckley residence and rang the doorbell. Mary Lou worked at Schiller and Smith while Finn, her husband, did odd jobs around town. Everyone called him Fix-it Finn and last year for his fiftieth birthday, the city council gave him three work shirts with that nickname embroidered on the front pocket. She noticed his pick-up parked in the driveway.

As he answered the door, she pulled out on of her fliers. "Hi, Finn. You have probably heard that I am the chairperson for the neighborhood watch teams in Scrub Oak."

"Yeah. But I don't think I can be counted on to patrol. Never know what my schedule will be like. People call me at all hours, you know."

"I do. However, I am not here to recruit. Frank told me he had seen a strange man carrying firewood a few days ago and noticed your side gate open."

"Really?" He stepped onto his porch and walked down the side steps. Wanda followed. He wiggled the gate. "It is warped, so sometimes it doesn't latch when ya close it." He chuckled. "Fix-it Finn I may be, but never seem to find the time to get to the honey-dos at my own house."

"Makes sense to me."

"Doesn't to Mary Lou." He sighed and yanked the privacy gate open. "Lookie there. Well, I'll be." He cocked his work cap back on his head.

The neatly stacked cord of wood had several pieces missing. Quite a few, as a matter of fact. It reminded Wanda of her childhood Lincoln Log constructions that always toppled.

"Do me a favor, Finn. Notify the police and file a report."

"You think I should? I mean, it seems kinda useless."

"You never know. Crime is crime."

He folded his arms over his chest. "You're right. Okay, I'll stop by there on the way to Anna's Antiques. Beverly has a ceiling fan that is screeching like a hoot owl."

Satisfied, Wanda canvased the neighbors on either side of Fir Boulevard, including the condos where Priscilla lived. No one recalled anything missing or any strangers in the area, except for a woman in the condos who thought she had left a blanket on the back seat of her car for her dog to lie on when they took a trip into the country to visit her sister. Now, it was not there. But it could've been in the wash pile, too. She'd check.

Wanda walked over to Evelyn's to solicit her help. After explaining what she'd uncovered so far, she accepted a cold tumbler of lemonade from her friend. She guzzled half the drink, not realizing how thirsty she'd become wandering the street in the summer heat.

"I think you need to take these details to Todd. You told him you would inform him of anything people notified out of the ordinary. Then let it alone. Escaped cons are nothing to fool with."

"You do make sense, Ev. I don't want him to poo-poo me, though. Wouldn't it be better to present him with hard evidence?"

"Whatcha gonna do? Wander in the woods, find the cave, and have a nice fireside chat with this Butch guy? Take a selfie with your phone and post it?"

"No, I guess not." She slithered into Evelyn's kitchen chair. "But finding the cave may not be such a bad idea. Maybe it isn't town lore. Arthur seemed convinced it existed."

Evelyn took the glass from her and felt her forehead. "Just checking for heatstroke. Otherwise, you are out of your mind."

Wanda brushed her hand away. "Stop. I am not saying I'd go alone."

"But you are saying you want to go. Who are you going to take with you? Betty Sue? I certainly am not going."

"Why not? You know how to handle a gun. You have your husband's old army issue in your nightstand, right?"

"Now wait a minute. How do you know that?"

"You told me when we thought there was a thief lurking around the resort. Said even in small towns you can never be too careful."

She harrumphed and dumped the leftover ice out of the

tumblers before placing them in the dishwasher.

Wanda patted her arm. "I must confess I had thought of getting one, too. As a widow it isn't a bad idea. Maybe one day you can show me how to use it."

"The state of Texas has courses online and the target ranges offer lessons as well. You have to sign a certificate saying you know how to use it before you can register to have a concealed weapon."

"Good to know." Wanda decided to segue into another topic. "I have an idea, Ev. Call Betty Sue. See if she can spend an hour or so this evening after dinner to help canvas the area. It's light outside until almost nine now. Maybe Hazel would like to help, too. Let's meet up here in an hour."

Fifty-two minutes later, the ladies arrived, eager to help. Wanda explained what had been going on. She also showed them a photo of Butch McClain.

Betty Sue's hand went to her mouth. "That's him. The strange man I saw in the grocer's."

"When?" Wanda's breath caught in her throat. So, he had been in Scrub Oak after all.

"Yesterday? No, the day before. I went early in the morning just as it opened. He came in soon after, and I knew he was not from around here. He appeared to not know where things were." She stared at the photo. "I thought he might be a tourist, but something about him made my body shiver. He barely said a word to Jodie, the checkout clerk, and seemed antsy as if he wanted to get out of there fast."

"You should have said something, Betty Sue." Wanda clicked her tongue and went to make copies of the photo for them to show their friends and neighbors. Then she returned and handed one to each of them. "We can divvy up the north end of Scrub Oak from the railroad tracks to the Ferguson mansion. Should be able to connect with almost everyone in our neighborhood north of downtown over the next two days and nights."

The ladies agreed they could at least cover a block or two before dark.

Wanda felt a bright warmth flow through her. "Wonderful. Thank you. Let's meet back here at 8:45. And Betty Sue. I'm sorry I got irritated."

"It's okay. I know you are fervent about this. The detail of seeing the man simply slipped my mind."

The ladies rose to leave. However, Evelyn lagged. She stopped at the door and turned back to Wanda.

"But . . ." Evelyn waggled her finger. "We are not going snooping in those woods after dark, right?"

"No, not tonight. Promise."

"Whatcha mean not tonight?"

Wanda ushered her outside. "Better get going. We only have an hour or so of sunlight left. See ya in a bit."

Evelyn narrowed one eye. Then she shook her head and left.

Chapter Twenty-One

When the sunset splashed oranges, purples, and pinks on the horizon, the four ladies met back at Wanda's house. With their group effort, they had already covered half of the northern section of town. Of course, not everyone had been home. They compared notes and checked off the ones they would canvas Saturday morning.

"I suggest we don't knock on doors too soon. No earlier than nine. Some people like to sleep in on weekends."

"Good point, Betty Sue. Anything weird to report so far, ladies?" Wanda tapped her pen on the kitchen table and cast her glance to each of her friends.

Betty Sue raised her hand, asking to speak, just as she had drummed into her students for decades. It made Wanda smile and the other two ladies giggle.

With cast-down eyes, she replied. "Well, I was just being polite."

"And I appreciate it." Wanda patted her arm. "Tell us what you found out."

"Well . . ." she wiggled in her chair. "It may be nothing,

but the Wickershams live across from Pecan Park, and one night last week, Elsa couldn't sleep. Blamed it on the pizza."

Head bobs and understanding "uh-huhs" spread around the table.

"She thinks she saw a man walking rather quickly through the park. The moon was half-hidden in the clouds, so she didn't have a clear view. You know, we should talk to the town council about putting in sensor lights in the trees. The streetlamps only hit the corners."

"Good idea. Let's make a note of that." Evelyn wrote it down.

Betty Sue's shoulders straightened. "And one block up on the same night, the Andrews' schnauzer kept barking about midnight, which was unusual because it always sleeps with them. Zee says it stood at the top of the stairs as if to warn someone to not open the front door. Her husband was out of town and it unnerved her."

"What night was that?" Wanda felt a coldness in her gut.

Betty Sue's eyes took on a sadness. "The night before the shooting."

"And neither family reported this?" Wanda raised her hands in the air. "Unbelievable."

"We've become too complacent in this town if you ask me." Evelyn crossed her arms over herself. "Scoff at any idea of foul play happening in our sleepy community. Convince ourselves it is nothing but our imaginations and go about our business."

"Or that it's *none* of our business, like my next-door neighbors." Hazel nodded at Wanda who agreed.

Evelyn reported that one couple on 9th thought they saw two men hurrying by late one night, but they couldn't recall the exact date. Recently, though. They seemed to be carrying something in their arms. "And two doors down, those neighbors noticed that a few yard tools had gone missing from their back yard. Thought maybe their teenage son had borrowed them to do some odd jobs for money. He cuts lawns during the spring and summer."

"Oh, that must be Jake." Betty Sue smiled. "He cuts mine, front and back for twenty dollars. Does a great job, too. Nice boy. Always did make good grades."

"Does he wear a flannel shirt?" Wanda cocked her head.

"In this heat? Heaven's no."

"Frank's stranger did. But then again, he said he thought it was an older man and could have been Butch McClain." She stood up. "Look. Let's create a calendar. I have an extra one in the den. That wildlife preserve sends me one each year. The hubs used to donate to them."

She returned and spread the month open. They took turns reporting who had seen what and when. A pattern began to develop, all within the past week since the burglary in Burleson. The four women silently stared at their findings, no one saying a word.

"I need to show this to Todd first thing in the morning."

Wanda blew a breath upwards toward her bangs.

"Agreed." Evelyn and Betty Sue responded in unison. Hazel nodded.

Wanda tore off the current month from the calendar. "I want to make printouts for each of the four neighborhood watch captains. That ought to convince the constituents of this town that we need to get organized."

Betty Sue raised her hand again. "Isn't this going to cast a shadow on our police department? Especially Todd since he has night patrol?"

Wanda thumped the pen against her cheek. "He can't be everywhere at once. If these are burglars, they would be making sure the coast was clear before they moved."

"True." Evelyn raised a finger.

"Even so, I might suggest that he change up his route now and then. He is a creature of habit." Wanda shrugged.

Evelyn grinned. "Like his aunt. You taught him well."

The other ladies, including Wanda, snickered.

The meeting broke up and Wanda walked everyone out. She watched as they each disappeared to their own homes. A quiet stillness fell over the town. The time of day that hung, just for a minute, between day and night always calmed her nerves. One by one streetlamps came on, casting their friendly glow to the sidewalks. Somewhere to the east, probably in Pecan Park, an owl hooted, momentarily hushing the cicadas' rhythmic hums.

How dare any thugs disturb her wonderful community. A righteous anger bubbled up into her heart. Carl was not right in shooting one of them, but in a way she understood. It was almost self-defense. If he had nicked the guy in the knees, not aimed for the chest, it would have been better. Perhaps the hunter in him whispered that one always shoots to kill, not maim. More humane to the animal. Except the victim had not been a deer.

Neither had Robert Stewart.

Could the two really be connected? Robert had bought the resort from Otto. Whose applecart had that action overturned?

She shook her head. Enough. Time to get a cup of chamomile tea, grab a handful of tea biscuits that she'd brought home from that specialty shop in Fort Worth, and watch the British whodunnit that came on at nine. *Pip-pip and all that*, as Watson used to say to Holmes.

A few minutes into the show, a loud bang echoed over the neighborhood. Then another.

Sophie jumped from her lap and dashed under the coffee table.

Wanda hesitated, wondering if she should join her pup or grab the baseball bat that she always leaned against the bedside table.

She saw shadows of people dash across her curtains. Curiosity got the best of her. She peered out onto a small crowd, some still dressed like her, others in pajamas and robes, hovering near her driveway. Evelyn's head turned toward her direction, and she beckoned Wanda outside.

Wanda walked as calmly as possible to the curb. After

all, as chairperson of the neighborhood watch she had to show decorum under pressure. Leaders always did.

"What's happening?"

Stanley Roberts, who lived with his wife and two kids on the other side of Evelyn, pointed toward the park. "Came from over there. We'd just returned from the movies in Cleburne and pulled in the driveway. Family is still locked in the car."

The pulsating siren of Todd's cruiser barreled around the corner and stopped. In a nano second, Chief Brooks screeched his car to a halt, a blue and red light swirling on top of his hood. Both men exited in a well-rehearsed dance, weapons drawn, knees slightly bent, arms extended, one hand flashing a beam of white light through the park in a crisscross fashion.

The beams revealed a clump sprawled on the ground near the swings.

Everyone gasped.

"Is it a body?" Stanley hissed the question through his teeth.

Beverly Newby swooned, and Frank Patterson huffed to catch her, with Evelyn's help.

Todd rushed back to the squad car and began to wind yellow tape around the trees bordering the playground.

All of the bystanders groaned.

Wanda stiffened her spine and walked across to meet him.

"Aunt Wanda, keep back. This is a crime scene." He

pointed over his shoulder with his head to the huddle of onlookers. "That goes for all of them, too."

"Do you know who it is?"

"I do." He stopped and pushed his hat back off his forehead. "But I can't reveal that yet. I can tell you it is not anyone who lives in Scrub Oak. You can spread that around town if you want."

She ignored the edge in his tone. "And Carl is still in jail. So, someone else must have killed this guy."

He huffed into his collar. "Not true. Seems he figured out how to escape about an hour ago."

Julie B Cosgrove

CHAPTER TWENTY-TWO

Wanda edged back over to the group of concerned neighbors. They all hushed their mumblings when she got within earshot.

"What did Todd say?" Evelyn stepped forward to greet her. One by one the others encircled her.

Being the center of attention unnerved her, but a sense of pride acted like a yeast in her heart, causing her courage to rise. Suddenly there was silence, as if the whole world hung on her next sentence.

Her senses became magnified. The streetlamps seemed brighter, the shadows harsher. The peach hand lotion Evelyn often used hit her nose. So did the dryer sheets Frank used. And a bit of the aftershave from Stanley mingled with residuals of Beverly's musky gardenia perfume.

"Okay, there's been another murder."

Everyone gasped, sucking the oxygen from the huddle.

Wanda held up her hands and pumped them to calm their nerves. "But it's not anyone who lives here in Scrub Oak. That's all that Todd could say for now."

"It's another of those burglars, isn't it?" Frank growled

the question. "I knew it."

"There is something else. It seems Carl Smithers escaped from jail tonight. I think we all need to go home and lock our doors."

As if she had said, *ready, get set, go* the crowd scattered, sprinting to safety. All but Evelyn.

"Can I come stay with you?"

"Sure, Evelyn. Of course. Bring Tweety. Sophie won't bug her." Tweety was her parakeet.

"Come with me?"

Wanda wrapped an arm over her shoulder and the two strolled up the wide driveway that separated their properties.

Evelyn's door stood wide open. Her friend halted so abruptly, Wanda had flashbacks of playing Red-Light Green-Light.

Why was Wanda associating people's moves with children's games? Because a body lay on the playground? She shook the thought away. "He's not going to be in there, hon. He made a dash to the woods or railroad tracks. Come on."

"You certain?"

"Of course. Carl isn't stupid enough to be trapped inside a house."

She heard Evelyn push a sigh of courage out her cheeks and edge up onto the porch. Wanda joined her as the two of them peered into the house.

Evelyn's cell phone screamed back at them, playing

"This Is the Way We Go to School." She reached for it. "Betty Sue. Hi, yes we're fine, but, wait until you hear . . ." Wanda harrumphed.

Just like that, Evelyn was over it. Wanda unhooked Tweety's cage from the stand and motioned to Evelyn. "Let's go. You can borrow one of my gowns and I have an extra toothbrush."

Evelyn nodded as she continued to fill in Betty Sue, who, it seemed, had already begun to dash over, via 11th Street. A longer way around, but it meant she avoided the park all together.

The two waited for her at Wanda's. In the meantime, Wanda texted Todd. *I may have some information for you. Been polling the neighbors to see who saw what."*

A thumbs up and then a frowning face emoji came back as his reply. She sighed and went to plug in the coffee machine. It was going to be a long night. Maybe she should pop some kettle corn, too?

The three women decided to pass the time watching the home improvement channel. They all agreed on which one the house-hunting couple should buy. It wasn't the one they chose, however. Evelyn sat back and folded her arms. "Idiots. That bungalow was a much better value."

"With less renovations needed, even though it was more expensive." Betty Sue shook her head.

Wanda sat forward. "Maybe that is why Robert Stewart bought the resort. Already fully staffed. Recently renovated. It may have seemed to be a great deal at the time."

"Why not make it public knowledge, though? It's not as if Otto's name brought any fame to the place." Evelyn scooted up on the sofa cushion and grabbed another handful of kettle corn.

"Out of fear of rejection by the community maybe? People didn't know him, other than the fact he was rich and Aurora had snared him in her neatly manicured claws."

"Wanda. Meow." Betty Sue clucked her tongue.

"I know, I have to work on my attitude toward her. Y'all are right. She is a widow just like we are. We should invite her over for Sunday dinner."

"Let's have it at my house." Betty Sue gave Wanda a sidelong glance. "Evelyn lives next door to you so it's like being on the edge of enemy territory."

Evelyn hooked a thumb in Betty Sue's direction. "She has a point."

"Great idea. And perhaps, during dinner, we can figure out a way to slip in why Robert bought the resort in such a hush-hush manner."

Her friends rolled their eyes and groaned.

An hour later, a very exhausted looking Todd knocked on her back door and then let himself in. "Aunt Wanda? I saw the lights were still on. Oh." He halted in the hallway when he noticed the three of them in the living room.

Wanda motioned him to join them. "We decided three's company in this case. Safety in numbers. Kettle corn?"

His frazzled expression changed into a tired grin. "No, thanks. A cup of coffee would be nice."

Wanda rose and he raised in his hand to stop her. "I'll get it. I know where everything is."

"Nice boy. You raised him well." Betty Sue smiled.

"He came out of my sister's womb that way. I can't take any credit."

They hushed when they heard his footfall returning and waited until he had eased his bones into one of the side chairs with a guttural groan.

"What can you tell us?"

Evelyn and Betty Sue both shot her a glare, but Wanda ignored it.

Todd set down his mug. "Not much, Aunt Wanda. We emailed the fingerprints and mug shot to Fort Worth. They have the state database so hopefully they can positively I.D. the victim. Naturally, he had no identification on him at the time."

"But you said you knew who it was."

He held up a finger. "I only meant that we had a good idea."

Wanda decided to let it slip. For now. "And Carl?"

"Still at large. The County Sheriff has called in the Texas Rangers to help in the man hunt. They'll find him."

"Wait." Wanda rubbed her temple. "How would Carl

have gotten a deer rifle?"

Todd shoved his hat back off his forehead. "Who told you that?"

A smirk eased over her face. She couldn't help it. "I heard the shots. I know what a deer rifle's discharge sounds like."

Todd leaned forward, his hands pressed to his knees. "And what were you doing at the time?"

"Watching a mystery on TV. Earlier that evening I'd been canvassing the neighbors along with Betty Sue, Hazel, and Evelyn. You see, Frank told me he saw a guy with a flannel shirt carrying away some fire logs from the Buckley's." She then told him about the man that the Wickershams lady saw a few nights back.

"The vic wore a flannel shirt." He took off his Stetson and massaged his temples. "Okay. You may as well know. I didn't exactly lie when I said the vic wasn't a resident of Scrub Oak."

"But . . .?" Wanda tilted her head toward him.

"He once lived here. I remember him. He was a legend of sorts. The guys would point to his picture in the hallway, you know where the class photographs are hung in chronological order?"

The three women nodded.

"A real thug, always in trouble with the principal. The notorious bad apple of the school who dropped out of sight. They used to make up stories about him to scare the cub scouts at campouts."

"Who?"

"Tommy Reynolds."

"What? But he was one of the boys in Colton's gang, which means he'd have been born around in 1968. Right, Betty Sue? That is what you calculated."

"That's correct."

"So?" Todd narrowed in on Wanda's face.

"He'd be in his early fifties by now. Similar in age to Butch McClain."

"That's right. But his legend lives on. Scrub Oak's own James Dean."

Wanda furrowed her brow. "But the report at the police station stated the other burglars were younger."

"Reports can be mistaken. The CCV cameras were a tad out of focus. They judged the age by the build and gait of the men they caught on film."

"Meaning a man in his fifties who had kept in shape could resemble a thirty-year-old."

"Exactly, Betty Sue." Todd sighed.

"See, ladies. It pays to eat right and exercise." She sat back with a nod of satisfaction.

Evelyn and Wanda glanced at each other, then waggled their heads. Betty Sue's logic didn't quite work itself out.

"Wait." Wanda snapped her fingers. "Todd, if you identified him as Tommy, why send off the fingerprints and mug shot?"

"To make sure, as I said. I mean the face resembles him but all I had to go by was my memory of a decades-old high school photo. Jim Bob recalls him, though he was in elementary school when Tommy was quietly expelled."

"So that's what happened to him." Betty Sue snapped her fingers. "Mrs. Tucker figured as much."

"Who?" Todd turned to her.

"An old teacher in a nursing home. We went to visit her."

Todd blew out a giant exhale. "Really, Aunt Wanda? You only just thought to tell me about that?"

Betty Sue and Wanda both studied their fingernails.

"I thought we had an understanding. You would share things with me. Not keep me in the dark." He leaned forward, putting his elbows on his knees. "And stop investigating."

Wanda opened her mouth to further explain. Then she stopped. A thought hit her out of the blue . . . again. "Wait. That would mean Carl recognized him, too. Could it be he took revenge because Tommy led his brother astray all those years ago?"

Todd leaned back and took a long sip of his coffee. Then he set the mug down with purpose. "Okay. That's one theory we are working on. I shouldn't tell you this, and I don't know why in Heaven's name I am. But since you ladies insist on snooping, you would probably figure it out anyway."

"What?" the three all replied in union, their spines erect and feet flat to the floor.

"The first victim, the one Carl supposedly shot that is

in the morgue?"

Betty Sue gasped. "Is Bubba Huffman."

"Bingo." Todd shot his forefinger at her. She was right on target.

Julie B Cosgrove

CHAPTER TWENTY-THREE

Wanda couldn't sleep. Todd had convinced her friends that it was safe to return to their homes, but the things he had revealed that night twirled in her brain like a smoothie in a blender. The whispering in her head telling her that Carl was not the one wouldn't go away, yet all the evidence pointed to him. And why would he escape if he were innocent? That stunt made him appear even more guilty.

She threw off her covers, padded to the desk, and got out a spiral notebook and pen. Back to the old-school way of doing things.

She wrote down the names of Carl, Colton, Bubba, Tommy, Otto, and Mr. Ferguson. Then off to the side she added Butch McClain and Robert Stewart. Then she sketched a timeline.

1981 – Carl and Colton's parents killed in a car accident and the boys adopted by the Arthurs.

1982 – oil bust and dairy farm sold. Colton off to military school? Tommy's dad worked on the dairy farm almost fifteen years. Now out of a job? What happened to the dad? Is it relevant?

1982 – Otto buys the land and builds the resort. Seems an odd time to do that during an economic bust like none other the state had ever seen. Why?

2019 – Robert Stewart buys the resort. Was killed in hunting "accident" within a few months of moving across the lake with Aurora. Has to be connected somehow.

2019 – Two months later Ferguson dies. Estate in probate. Any connection??

2020 – robbery in Burleson. Tommy, Bubba, and Butch hang out at old Ferguson's. Tommy and Bubba killed.

Where is Butch? AND CARL????

She thumped the pen on the paper and read her notes again. Too many holes. Too many loose ends. And the feeling still gnawed at her gut that Carl Smithers could not be a murderer. Who then? Butch McClain? Lurking in the shadows behind Carl the first time and now the perp this time? Made some sort of sense.

Maybe Butch helped Carl escape and followed him to meet with Tommy. Or, he let Carl escape and then killed Tommy so he could have all the jewelry to himself and finger Carl in the process. It would seem a reasonable thing for a hardened criminal to do—make sure someone else got the blame.

Whatever the scenario, Wanda bet Butch and Carl had words with each other.

Wait. Words. The inscription in her dictionary from Todd. *We will always have words with each other.*

The Scrabble letters.

She scurried off the bed, rousing Sophie who groaned and padded after her into the kitchen.

Flicking on the light over the sink, Wanda squinted until her eyes adjusted. Then she made a cup of hot herbal tea and pulled the Scrabble board down to the kitchen table.

Then she returned to the bedroom, snatched the notebook, and waddled in her bare feet back to the kitchen. Head resting in her hand, she wrote down the words. Maybe some of the others they had spelled were clues as well?

Or none of them were.

Cave, bushes, auto, shot. Jewels, perp, lying, woods. Then she looked at the other ones. *Candy, zero, reduce, panel, under, swing, park.*

Wait, now "swing" and "park" made sense. There was a cave, near the woods. Jewels were stolen, Carl was the perp(?), two men had been shot now, and one was lying by the bushes leading into the woods.

So, the rest had to be clues. They simply had to be. But "candy", "zero", "reduce" and "panel"? She yawned and stretched the kink from her spine, then she got up and opened her back door. Sitting on the porch she listened to the peaceful night sounds of a small town fast asleep. Sophie plodded out and rested her chin on Wanda's foot.

As she bent to scratch her pet's velvety ears, Wanda gazed into the darkness, barely dimmed by the golden glow of the streetlight.

The answers lay out there somewhere. If the police

found Carl, or Butch, perhaps they would be able to discover them. She certainly didn't plan join in the man hunt. The two were probably halfway to Canada or crossing into Mexico by now anyway.

She rubbed her eyes and pulled her nightgown around her knees. Bowing her head, she prayed that no more killings would happen in her community, that these tragedies would be used for good—a catalyst to rev up interest in the neighborhood watch, and that her life would get back to normal, whatever that was.

Then she felt Sophie's cold nose rub her ankle. Patting her pooch, she went back inside, bolted the door—something she rarely ever did—and then headed down the hall to her bed, the fast clicks of puppy dog nails following behind her.

The next morning, a chirpy cardinal, perched on the oak tree limb outside of her bedroom window, woke her up. Wanda let Sophie out, fixed breakfast, and listened to the morning news out of the DFW Metroplex just in case they mentioned any of the events that had happened in Scrub Oak. They did.

"And in other news, the sleepy little town of Scrub Oak, southeast of Cleburne, has had two murders in the past week. Police will not say the two are related at this time, however, the local citizen accused of the first murder escaped from jail less than an hour before the second one occurred. The suspect is still at large. A sketch of his face can be found on our website. If you think you see this man, tweet us or call 9-1-1. And now here is Mike with today's forecast . . ."

Great.

The phone began ringing at a little after eight. Wanda must have received fifteen calls over the next hour about the shooting, asking her what she was doing about forming the watches. Part of her prayers answered. Time to get busy.

She spent the rest of the day canvassing those she had not reached Friday, and then contacting the people who had signed up to participate in the neighborhood watch. She secured the fellowship hall at the church for an emergency meeting at seven that night. She decided not to involve Officer McIntyre, but she did phone the police station and let them know.

No one she queried had seen or heard anything unusual. At noon, Betty Sue, Hazel, and Evelyn reported that they had not gleaned any more useful information from the people they spoke with either. Maybe it was because these people worked during the day or everyone had become tight-lipped, not wishing to get involved. Especially the younger ones. They spent all their time with their eyes glued to lighted screens on their phone, computer monitors, or tablets. No one ever caught up on the local gossip and news over the back fence anymore.

Before she left for the meeting Saturday evening, she fed Sophie, let her out for her nightly constitution, and then took a picture of the Scrabble board. Next, she sluffed the tiles into the draw bag, and put the game away. The first clues had been discovered to be relevant only as an afterthought. Perhaps it would be the same with the last ones.

Who knew? Maybe they were just words.

When she arrived at the church, several people had already gathered. She had one-hundred percent attendance by the time the meeting started, minus any of the police. Oh, well. She hoped that meant they were busy with the manhunt.

She organized everyone into four groups, as the expert had suggested. Each group voted for a captain. Neighbors, if they spotted anything suspicious, were supposed to report to the watchers and the watchers to the captains. Wanda and the captains were to stay in contact, and she was then to report any such activity to the police. Of course, in dire cases, anyone could bypass the system and dial 9-1-1.

Everyone exchanged phone numbers up the line. Wanda placed the four captains on speed dial. Luckily, all of the watchers had cell phones and emails. She'd worried about that considering many of them were retired.

That night she typed up a directory, dividing the four quadrants, and emailed the list to everyone. By the time the news came on at ten, she was too tired to concentrate on it.

Instead, she crawled under the covers, reviewed her

Bible study lesson one more time, said her prayers, and let her head sink into her pillow. But she flipped and flopped all night like a fish on a riverbank. She dreamt she was walking by the lake when she heard weeping. A disheveled Aurora sat barefoot on the bank in a muddied pink chiffon dress. Her shoulders heaved as she buried her bleached-blonde head in her hands. On them were tattooed the words "lonely" and "lost" in Scrabble tiled fashion.

That did it.

After church the next morning, she cornered Betty Sue and Evelyn. "Let's meet to organize the invite for Aurora, make it a brunch for next Saturday. I have been thinking we should invite Hazel and Beverly, too. They are both widows as well. That way it won't seem so awkward. And six will fit around Betty Sue's dining room table anyway. We can call it the Scrub Oak Widow's Society."

"Great idea." Betty Sue peered into her face. "You okay? Your eyes look as if they are going to sink into your cheeks."

"Didn't sleep well."

Evelyn let out a "pfft" sound. "Who has? Carl is still at large. Every dog bark jolted me out of my slumber last night."

"You need more iron, and probably magnesium. I put vitamin and mineral drops in my water every morning." Betty Sue laid a hand on Evelyn's arm.

"Your water?"

"Yes. Water." Betty Sue turned to her. "Didn't you

know you should drink at least eight ounces upon rising every day? It is good for the ol' ticker." She patted her chest.

"I do drink eight ounces. In my coffee mug."

"Wanda Lee Warner, really." Betty Sue scoffed at her. "Why do I even try?"

She tromped down the hallway, her head in the air.

Evelyn turned to Wanda. "Now you did it."

"What?" She picked up her Bible from the pew. "She'll be over it by the time she pulls into her driveway."

"How'd ya know that?"

"Because I am going to text her to help me pick out the invites at Kay's Flowers tomorrow morning and also decide on the floral bouquet for her table."

"Ah, she'll like that."

"We'll use my grandmother's high tea set. It will be fun, right?"

Evelyn shrugged. "It will be interesting. Guess there isn't a chance of ordering Irish stew from the Hook & Owl, then?"

Wanda chuckled. "For a moment, I thought you were serious."

From the expression Evelyn wiped from her face, perhaps she had been.

"Evelyn, this has to be girlie. Besides, it is summer. Too hot for stew."

"Oh, okay." Her tone drooped. "What were you thinking of?"

"Iced raspberry tea. Crustless sandwich points, fresh

fruit, scones from Sally's. We could have tarragon chicken salad on Batavia lettuce boats." She knew Evelyn liked chicken salad, especially the way Wanda made it.

"Okay, count on me for getting the scones and fruit. Brownies, too. And definitely go with the chicken salad. You make a great one with the pecans, celery, and grapes in it. Oh, and how about your deviled eggs?"

"Done. I'll tell Betty Sue to make the sandwiches. She makes a great homemade palmetto cheese. And some with cucumber with creamed cheese would be nice. We'll make it a real old fashioned tea."

"As long as we don't have to wear white laced gloves." Evelyn waved goodbye.

Wanda's footsteps lightened. She almost skipped to her car. It felt nice to have something else besides crime and murder on her mind.

Then she looked across the street and saw Todd dash to his squad car, rev it up, and peal out of the back lot of the police station.

Her hand froze on her car fob. He didn't use his siren or lights. Why the rush?

Should she follow?

Definitely.

Julie B Cosgrove

Chapter Twenty-Four

Wanda knew if she tailed Todd, he'd figure it out as soon as he glanced a few times in his rearview mirror. So, when she saw him turn north on 8th, she took 7th instead since Scrub Oak was basically laid out in a grid pattern. Through the side yards between the houses and off the side streets she could spot him as he continued north toward the Ferguson Mansion, she gathered.

She called up her digital system to ring the captain of the northern quadrant, Melissa Suntych, who was a local artist and animal rescuer. She also attended Holy Hill but went to the earlier service, so even though she lived on Woodway at the edge of town she should be home by now.

"Melissa. Glad I caught you. Listen, Todd is high-tailing it up 8th as we speak. See if you can see if he turns on Woodway . . . yes, in his squad car. There is something going on."

She then called the middle quadrant's captain, Vlad, Zelda's hubby, a cabinetry and furniture maker who lived on Pecan. "Be on the lookout. Todd may be turning in your direction. He is in his cruiser going pretty fast."

There. She had the bases covered, so to speak. If someone had reported a suspicious man lurking, she'd know about it soon enough. Her eyebrows crinkled. Wait. If there was danger in the area, wouldn't the police be obligated to contact the neighborhood watch to spread the word? To secure safety of the citizens, of course. She needed to ask Officer McIntyre about it and have him contact Chief Brooks. Seemed to her the word "communication" meant information should pass along a two-way street.

Within a few minutes, Vlad called back. Todd was helping to herd Mrs. Porter's fifteen chickens out of the neighbors' front yards and back into their backyard coop. She had mistakenly left the latch unhooked when she gathered the eggs. It wasn't until the basset hound next door began frantically barking that she noticed the empty coop. She had never fenced in her property.

Wanda sat back and sighed. Small town stuff. What did she expect?

She laughed at herself and headed home.

The next morning at ten, she met Betty Sue at Kay's. Wanda stopped her as they entered the shop. "Betty Sue. Sorry about the snarky coffee mug reference yesterday after church."

Betty Sue swatted it away. "I can be a bit of a nag about your health. It's only because I love you, dear friend."

Wanda nudged her with her shoulder. "I know. Back at ya."

"These are nice. I like the garden scene on them with the bistro table set for two." Betty Sue held one up a painted invitation from the turnstile.

"Okay. Let's get three. You, Evelyn, and I don't need one. I will drop off Hazel's and Beverly's in their mailboxes if you drop off Aurora's."

"Wanda, what if Aurora declines?"

"Well then, at least we made the effort and the five of us can have a good time anyway."

"True. Though chicken salad is a tad fattening. So are deviled eggs."

"Betty Sue. It's a party."

"True. However, I plan on using low-carb whole grain bread for the cucumber sandwiches and cloud bread for the palmetto cheese."

"Cloud bread?"

"It's gluten free, Wanda. Fluffy and tasty." She wandered over to the cut flowers. "Don't scrunch up your nose. You'll like it."

They decided on pink tea roses and white daisies with baby's breath and fern leaves for the center decoration. Kay even offered to bring it to over early Saturday morning so it would be fresh. "I think what you are planning is the greatest idea. You widows need to be there for each other."

Her lip curled a bit downward.

Wanda smiled back. She hated the awkward sympathy married women gave widows. Always had. No one knew what it was like to have half of yourself ripped away and stuck inside a coffin until it happened to them. She missed her hubby every single day, though the pain had dissipated slowly, like a breath does on a cold windowpane. The sorrow had retreated to a background comfort somehow, like a friendly shadow to remind her she had been loved.

Plus, God had been faithful to remind her of His presence ever since the numbness of grief had begun to morph into sharp prickles of loss. She could not fathom what widowhood would be like for someone without faith.

Betty Sue gave her a soft smile as if she thought the same thing. Maybe she did. They had known each other long enough and had both experienced death's rude descent on a couple. They paid for the cards and flowers and then left.

As Wanda walked Betty Sue to her car, her friend laughed. "I guess you heard about the chicken escapade yesterday?"

"Yes." Wanda groaned. "Poor Todd. The things police do for their town."

"Not all glamorous and gun-slinging is it?"

"Nope. Praise God. But I can't shake off the eerie cloak of dread that keeps wanting to wrap over my shoulders. Two suspects are still at large. And one, if not both, are murderers."

Betty stopped with her hand on her car handle. "I know. And I am sorry. I know you wanted Carl to be innocent."

Wanda glanced down to the sidewalk and nodded.

"Thank you, Wanda, for organizing the neighborhood watch teams. Truly, one of your best ideas ever." Betty Sue squeezed her shoulder and then opened the car door.

As her best friend drove away, Wanda felt a surge of purpose erupt through her veins. The sooner Carl and Butch were captured, the better. Then maybe everyone in Scrub Oak could sleep soundly again.

Common sense dictated the pair had fled far away. So why did the notion that they were still hiding out somewhere in town keep niggling at her brain?

She slammed on her brakes and pulled over. The cave. That's it. She had to find the cave. Something told her everything else revolved around it.

She got out her phone and texted Evelyn. *Ever gone spelunking?*

Not since a field trip to Cascade Caverns on I35 for my college geology class. They had just discovered a new cavern. We got dirty, but it was fun. Why?

I want to find the Ferguson cave.

Wanda . . .

The texting stopped. Wanda stared at the screen. The cursor line blinked back at her. Then she saw the next message appear.

OK. But let's wait until next Saturday night.

Long time away. Why?

If we are arrested for trespassing and leave Betty Sue to host the whole thing, she'll kill us.

Wanda threw back her head and whooped. *If we do it tonight, we'll be out of jail by then.* She ended with a winky emoji.

OK. Deal. But let's do it tomorrow night. I call my kids on Mondays. Will nine o'clock work?

To her surprise, Aurora phoned her and accepted the invitation the next morning. Betty Sue had put Wanda's phone number as the RSVP.

Bewildered, Wanda asked Betty Sue why she had done it.

"Transparency. I listed us as co-hosts of the Scrub Oak Widow's Society. I didn't want her to stomp out when she saw you perched in my living room."

"Oh. Good thinking."

"For an icebreaker, I thought I might look through the archives for pictures of our hubbies. I can definitely track down some for Robert and Aurora from the Dallas society pages."

Wanda chuckled. "No problem there."

Betty Sue cleared her throat. "And I can find ours in our yearbooks since we met our guys in high school."

The memory of that junior prom danced through

Wanda's thoughts as if it had happened a few months prior. She and Betty Sue had double dated. Both of their husbands-to-be went to school in Cleburne. They had met at church camp the previous summer. A sweet sadness flowed over her. "We were two blessed gals, my friend."

"Yes, we were. I still have a photo of us on our wedding day on my nightstand."

"I know I have a scrapbook from our wedding and engagement party. We can use some of those."

"Good. I'll see what I can scratch up for everyone else. Beverly grew up in Arlington and Hazel is from around here. In fact, she may have gone to Cleburne High School with our men. Evelyn will be the hard one though. Where did she meet hers?"

"At UT in Austin. Check out the years 1974-1978. They were both in the band."

"Got it."

"Of course, we could ask everyone to bring their own."

Betty snickered. "It would save time, but I've got plenty of leads now. I don't mind scrounging them up as a surprise. I need a new project."

She did? It seemed Betty Sue always kept busy. Wanda shrugged it away and went about her daily chores.

She had to admit working on something other than solving crimes felt like a fresh cool breeze just before a rain shower on a scorching summer day. So, to keep from thinking about caves and murders, she decided to rearrange some of the shelves in her pantry and check for expired dates. That led to her weeding through her clothes closet and bagging for charity some items she had not worn in a year or so. A few she decided to hang on to for another year just in case.

Before she knew it, Sophie was whimpering at her empty bowl. Dinner time.

That evening, over a nice cup of tea, she flipped through her wedding album and chose two photos as well as one of their engagement pictures. Running a finger down her husband's face, she could almost feel his dimples again.

The phone rang, with a very out of breath Betty Sue on the other end.

"What is it?"

"You'll never guess. I went to the library and checked out several old yearbooks. People had donated them, you know."

"Right."

"Anyway, I found one from Carl. And guess what. There is an inscription under Aurora's picture. It's in her handwriting, I guess. It says, "I won't forget you. Love, Candy."

"Candy?"

"Don't you remember? She was always sucking on tootsie roll pops. Guess that was her nickname."

"Now that you mention it. Wasn't there also an old song called *Candy Girl*."

Yes, by Frankie Valli. There is a reference to it in the yearbook. Seems the kids used to hum that when she came down the hall."

"Knowing Aurora, she probably liked the attention." Then Wanda shuddered. "Wait. Candy was one of the words on the Scrabble board."

Betty Sue's sigh came through the phone. "I know. That's why I called."

Julie B Cosgrove

CHAPTER TWENTY-FIVE

Wanda felt uncomfortable about this whole brunch thing now. Maybe they should cancel?

But that seemed silly. The reference to Aurora's nickname on the Scrabble board could be totally coincidental. She had overreacted to Wanda's snooping at the resort and tried to tarnish Wanda's good standing in the town but that didn't make her an accessory to a crime.

On the other hand, what if she had married Robert for his money, come back to Scrub Oak, and fell in love again with Carl? Did he kill Robert so they could be together? Did she help plot it?

Wanda shook her head. Don't be ridiculous. Besides, the fact she accepted the invitation meant something, right?

Right.

Unless she accepted so she could keep tabs on them for Carl.

No. Not worth considering. Carl probably thought Wanda remained on his side. And, deep in the corner of her gut, she did. Even if all the evidence pointed to the opposite,

209

her little voice said Carl couldn't be a cold-blooded killer of two, if not three, people. It was someone else. But who?

She chided herself and caught up on some emails before taking a bath and getting ready to watch an old game show on TV.

Then Melissa texted her.

Drove down Woodway on my watch. Saw two shadowy figures duck into the woods. What do I do?

Nothing more. I will call Todd. Thanks.

But Todd didn't answer. Wasn't he on patrol tonight?

Wanda bit her lip. Where could he be?

Then she stared at her reflection in her phone. Think like a neighborhood watch chairperson, not a doting aunt, Wanda. Protocol.

She called the police station and reported it to Jim Bob.

"I am being a nosy aunt. Where's Todd?"

"At his apartment in Lakeview. I am taking his shift."

"Oh. Okay, thanks." She wondered why. Had he been reprimanded? She decided to call his landline.

"Everything is fine, Aunt Wanda. I had to give my testimony to the county judge in Cleburne today since I was first on the scene last Friday night. Tons of paperwork. Protocol for a murder investigation. I didn't get back until after dinner."

Now Wanda felt stupid. Policemen had so many duties she didn't know about. "Well, I called Jim Bob because one of my watch captains reported two shadowy figures dashing into the woods from Woodway."

"We have had trouble with squatters hitching on the railroad cars lately. Signs of the times. And of course, kids are always trying to get free rides to Fort Worth and back."

"So, you don't think . . ."

"Aunt Wanda." His sigh came through loud and clear. "If Carl was idiotic enough to remain in town, don't you think we'd have figured that out by now?"

"Of course." His reprimanding tone stabbed her in the heart.

"Look, it's been a very long day. I am tired and a bit on edge. I didn't mean to . . ."

"It's okay. Get some sleep."

She clicked off and stared out the window. Surely Carl would be long gone unless he had a very good hiding place. Someplace very few people know about . . .

Like the cave.

She and Evelyn planned to meet and explore the grounds of the Ferguson mansion. Assuming the existence wasn't a local folklore but an actual place once used for bootlegging, perhaps it would be large enough for two men to hide out inside. But if they were, it would not be wise for two elderly women to be traipsing around trying to locate the entrance to their hidey hole.

She didn't dare call Todd again, but could it wait until their Thursday morning Scrabble game? Something told her it could not.

She went to her prayer chair, otherwise known as the easy chair, where she often read her devotionals or studied for her Bible study lessons and asked for wisdom. After a minute, Adam Arthur's name came to her.

Was 9:25 at night too late to call?

Probably. Tomorrow she would head to the firehouse.

Wanda yawned as she headed down the short hall to her bedroom. A banging on her door halted her in her tracks. Who on earth?

She tiptoed back to the living room and heard the banging again. Definitely at her front door. It wouldn't be Evelyn or Betty Sue. They would call, text, or come in the back. They knew where she kept the key.

She tiptoed to the peephole and closed one eye to peer through the miniature shaft. A distorted man's face appeared, staring back at her.

"Wanda? You awake?"

She recognized the voice. "Adam Arthur?"

"Yes. May I come in?"

What on earth? His name had just been on her mind. A shiver flowed through her as if an angel had blown on her neck. Godly serendipities rarely happened to her.

She unbolted the front door and let him in. "No, it isn't too late. Are you all right?"

He appeared disheveled in sweatpants and a t-shirt. His hair was mussed under a terry cloth head band.

"I was taking a late night stroll. I do that when I can't sleep. Ate at the Hoot and Owl too late I guess." He motioned if he could enter further into the room.

Wanda motioned for him to sit on the sofa.

"No, I am a tad sweaty. I won't stay long, It's just, I thought Todd might be here."

"No. Why?"

The fire chief ran his hand over his head. As he did, Wanda noticed it shake a bit.

"I swear I just saw, but it couldn't be."

"Who?"

"Carl. As I walked down 6th from my house on Pecan, I saw him leaving Aurora's out the side door and head toward the edge of the woods."

She placed both hands firmly on his shoulders, which meant she had to stand on her tiptoes. "Carl, you need to call Jim Bob, now. He's on duty."

The man glanced to the ground and nodded. "He's my brother though."

"He is a wanted criminal who escaped from jail."

"Right." He bobbed his head quickly as if to let common sense settle into his brain. He plopped down on her couch and gazed at her face. "I can't believe he'd do these things. Colton, maybe. But Carl? Never."

"I know. Carl was always the quiet one, the good one." She raised her hands in front of her. "I know. He became bolder and more fervent, especially since he bought that gas station and started up the used car lot. But it seemed to me it was more misplaced enthusiasm. As if he'd finally found his niche in life and wanted everyone to know it."

Adam agreed. "This is tearing up my gut." He massaged his slightly protruding belly.

"That or the Irish stew?"

His mouth formed a tiny smile. "Possibly both. Well, thank you. I'll pray about what to do."

He rose and she did as well.

His expression became sheepish. "Guess I better get home. Wife is visiting her sister in Houston and if people saw me leaving your house at this hour, well, I can hear the tongues wagging."

Wanda knew she blushed. She waved it away. "Adam. Really."

He chuckled and opened the front door.

"Goodnight, Wanda."

"Goodnight." She held the door slightly ajar so Sophie wouldn't dash out. "And Adam? Let me know what happens."

He raised his hand in response as he walked down the steps from her porch.

Then her brain kicked in. "Wait. Adam."

He halted and turned back. "Yeah."

She came toward him. "That cave business. It is real, right?"

"Yes."

"Do you know where the entrance is?"

"From outside or inside?"

CHAPTER TWENTY-SIX

Wanda stammered. "W-what?"

"There is the outside entrance into the cave, obviously, though I don't know where it is. But I do know it connects to the wine cellar in the basement of the Ferguson mansion. Of course, the door is bolted so no one can get into the cave."

"You know this for a fact?"

Adam Arthur shifted his weight to the left foot. "Ten years ago, there was a kitchen fire. It started from a gas leak behind the stove."

"Why, yes. I vaguely remember that."

"The pipes run into the basement where the wine cellar sits. I had to inspect the line for leaks afterwards with the insurance company adjustor and we saw the door half hidden behind a wine rack." He walked back up her steps to the porch. "That's when old Mr. Ferguson told us about his pappy's bootleggin' cave. I knew then that Carl had not been lying about his brother and those two hoodlums hanging out in it."

"Adam. You know those two hoodlums were shot dead, right?"

"When?"

"Bubba in the woods by Carl, or so it's supposed. And Tommy in the park a few nights ago."

He wobbled backwards until he found a porch post to steady himself. "We need to tell Chief Brooks. Now."

"We?"

He patted his hips. "No pockets. Left my phone at home."

"Ah." Wanda went inside to grab her phone. "Okay. You can use mine. But you do the talking. Brooks thinks I am a meddling old lady who sticks her nose in his business."

When a gruff Chief Brooks answered, Wanda explained that Arthur had spotted something suspicious while jogging and didn't have his phone so he knocked on her door and asked to borrow hers. Before he could respond she handed the instrument to the fire chief.

Adam told Brooks what he thought he saw, then he said, "uh-huh" and walked back down the porch steps onto the sidewalk out of earshot.

Her curiosity itch needed scratching, but Wanda resisted the urge to follow him so she could eavesdrop. Instead, she took deep, cleansing breaths and waited on the stoop.

Finally, Adam walked back and handed her the phone. "Well?"

"He wants me to meet him at the mansion and show

him this entrance from the wine cellar. He is getting the key from the attorneys."

"Very well. Let me put on some shoes." She wiggled her bare toes. Wanda rarely wore shoes at home during the summer.

"Why are you coming?"

Wanda pointed to her garage. "I've got the car?"

His round cheeks darkened. "I guess I was going to jog up there. Where is my head?'

"In your heart. You are a rescuer. That's your nature. And you are also a law-abiding citizen. Thus, you are conflicted."

He tapped his temple. "You are a wise lady, Wanda Lee Warner. No wonder my wife thinks the world of you."

"She does?" His wife was a successful owner of the beauty salon chain known as A Cut Above, with branches in Cleburne, Burleson, Keene, and Alvarado as well as locally. And she sat on the board of the county's chamber of commerce.

Warmth rush to her cheeks. She turned to go back inside. Slipping her feet into some old oxfords, she grabbed her purse and phone. Then she went to the garage and clicked the button to open the double doors.

Adam stood on the other side waiting for her. She clicked the car door fob. Adam came around an opened the driver's side for her.

"I appreciate this, Wanda. But I don't want you to get in danger."

"I won't." She got in and clicked her belt but didn't start the ignition.

"What's wrong?'

"Now *I'm* conflicted. I promised Todd if I learned about anything of importance, I would keep him in the loop. But I don't want to jeopardize his career."

Adam touched her arm. "What does your heart tell you?"

Wanda sighed and pulled out her phone, telling it to call her nephew. Then she put it on speaker.

A very groggy gruff voice answered on the other end. "Aunt Wanda, you okay?"

"I am. But listen. I have Adam Archer here with me. He has just called Chief Brooks. I will let him explain."

Adam leaned closer to the phone and once again relayed what he thought he saw.

They heard bed springs creak and two feet thud across the floor. Then a drawer screech open. "I'll meet you there. But Aunt Wanda?"

"Yes, Todd?"

"I want you to stay in the car. Do you hear me?"

"I hear you."

"Good." He hung up.

Wanda and Adam drove toward the mansion, but she stopped at the entrance to the lane. "What if they see us coming?"

"They will hightail it out of there through the cave and disappear again in the woods."

"Right. Not what we want." She cut her headlights. The almost full moon hung in the sky above the mansion as if suspended between the bookend chimneys like a tightrope walker. Its soft glow cast across the lane, elongating the shadows.

Wanda spun the car around and headed back toward Woodway to warn Todd.

As she turned right from 8th, they saw his cruiser heading in the opposite direction. The red and blue police lights on his rack flashed and the whoop-whoop of his siren blared as he did a 180 turn.

"Oh, great." Wanda pulled over and stopped as he edged up behind her car. He opened his door and strolled to her driver side in his patrol-on-duty walk. He wore jeans and a polo shirt, but his badge and gun hung from his belt.

She rolled down the window and waved at him.

Todd cocked his Stetson back off his forehead, flicked on his flashlight, and peered inside the driver's window.

The sudden white light hurt Wanda's eyeballs. She used her arm to shield them. "Todd what's with the light?"

"Where are yours?"

She had forgotten to turn the headlights back on. Adam leaned over. "Hey, Todd. We turned them off in case the burglars were on the grounds and saw them."

He nodded. "Hello, Adam. Thought you were meeting Chief Brooks."

"I am still taking Adam to meet him. I wanted to flag you down and tell you to turn off your headlights as well."

Todd straightened up. "I don't think they would care since we are not on the property."

Two cars passed by, and in the moonlight, Wanda saw them rubberneck.

Just great. Now the whole town would know she had been pulled over by her nephew. By noon people would be saying she was speeding, or drunk, or who knows what. Her reputation as neighborhood watch chairperson would be ruined.

Wanda pictured the whispers and shaking heads as she walked down the street to the grocer's or to Sally's. Would Betty Sue and Evelyn be ashamed to be seen with her?

She had a new appreciation of how her sister must have felt. She should call her. Maybe visit her—for a few months.

Todd tapped his fingers on the open window edge. "Okay, Aunt Wanda. I'll give you a warning. But I want you to go home. Adam, you come with me."

Adam jumped from the passenger seat and headed back with Todd to the squad car.

Wanda watched in her rearview mirror as they got in and turned to head back to the mansion. She thumped the steering wheel, her pride bruised. How dare Todd dismiss her like that.

She wiped a tear from forming in the corner of her eye and then clicked on her headlights. But as she waited to turn around, a thought hit her, as they often did.

Adam didn't know where the entrance to the cave lay, just that it existed. The woods, though only five acres deep, were dense with oak, cedar-elms and ash trees. It could take days to find the entrance.

They needed manpower. Time to rally the troops. Wanda pulled up to Hazel's house, edged into her driveway, and stopped. The windows on the first floor still shown with light. Thank goodness she was a night owl.

Wanda dialed her number. "Hey, Hazel. I need your help. Can you put on a pot of coffee?"

Julie B Cosgrove

Chapter Twenty-Seven

After she explained everything to Hazel, Wanda texted each of the four evening neighborhood watch captains to come ASAP to Hazel's house. Despite the late hour, they arrived within ten minutes. All had been doing their patrol at the time. What she didn't expect was that they'd each show up with another neighborhood patrol person and also a loaded weapon.

Then again, this was Texas. Kids as young as four used cacti as target practice for their BB guns. Up until recently it was not uncommon for boys, and some girls, to pull into the school parking lot after an early morning dove hunt, rack their shotguns in the truck, and then walk to class.

Hunting was part of a Texan's DNA. Most of these people probably carried weapons in their vehicles, a habit passed down when their daddies lived in even more rural areas and feared stepping out of the car onto a rattle snake or copperhead.

Hazel stepped up to the plate as the perfect hostess. They were greeted with the aroma of freshly brewed coffee and warm chocolate chip cookies.

Wanda held the brief meeting in the living room. She explained about the cave.

"Where is it?" Ray O'Malley removed his cap and scratched his head. "Never heard of it until now."

The others all agreed they had not either.

"Arthur is not sure, but obviously, it is well-hidden since after all of these decades it has been a secret."

Ray raised his hand. "What if we find it?"

"When." Wanda held up a finger. "When we find it. Because we must, tonight."

Everyone nodded and murmured in agreement.

She quieted them with her slightly raised voice. "You all should have my cell phone number since I just texted you to come here. Text me in reply and tell me approximately where you are if you stumble upon the entrance. I will contact the police who are also searching."

Everyone checked their phones. Then they divided into pairs. Wanda joined Melissa and Jerry Suntych. He had been a county bailiff before retiring.

"One more thing." She glanced at each face. "Be safe. Please. The last thing this town needs is another shooting. Now let's pray before we head out."

Everyone stood, formed a circle, and bowed their heads. Then they walked across the street and fanned out in pairs, each taking a quadrant of the woods. Wanda led the Suntychs to the most southern part, nearest to Aurora's house. To think the cave extended that far from the mansion was a stretch, no pun intended, but she had read that some priest holes in England measured up to a quarter mile long. Being this far south reduced her chances of coming across Adam and Todd anyway.

But what if one of the other teams ran into them?

She shook that thought away. She didn't have time to worry over it. If it happened, she'd handle it then. After all, she told Todd that she had heard him tell her to stay in the car. She never agreed to do so.

They walked along in silence, Jerry showing them the hunting skill about stepping flat-footed to avoid the crackling of twigs and leaves. The threesome searched under bushes, watched for any upturned ground around boulders, and even searched around the humongous roots of the old cypress trees closer to the lake's bank. Nothing.

After twenty minutes Wanda stopped and checked her phone for the umpteenth time. Not one message. She plopped on a log and sighed.

Melissa joined her.

"Don't get discouraged. It must be really well hidden to have gone undiscovered for this long. I mean, the way the kids roam these woods, you'd have thought one of them would have discovered it."

"That is exactly what has me puzzled. Why has it not been? Even Chief Archer thought it a wives' tale until he saw the entry in the mansion that led to the cave."

Jerry stood quietly nearby, his eyes scanning the woods as if protecting them.

Wanda followed his gaze to the clearing. From there she could detect the security lights on Aurora's property. How involved was she in all of this? Had she been supplying them with food and necessities for the past week? Why?

The thought of Carl and her possibly doing away with Robert Stewart returned. But until tonight all Wanda had as proof was a thirty year-old note in a yearbook. How many people ever stayed in love with a high school heartthrob anyway?

Even less believable would be the cheerleader Aurora having feelings for the wallflower Carl. There had to be another connection . . .

The fear that this might be all a huge mistake crawled into her throat. What if no one had been in the Ferguson mansion at all? And even if they found the entry to the cave, it didn't mean they would find anything, or anyone in it.

What did she expect? To walk in on Carl and Butch splitting up the jewels around a kerosene camping stove?

She rubbed her temples. If this ended up a bust, moving out of town would definitely be her only option—like to Honduras, maybe Australia.

"Brain working overtime?"

She noticed Melissa studying her. "Maybe. Guess we should head on." As she rose and brushed herself off, it finally hit her . . . again. Why did these thoughts always come out of nowhere? Divine intervention?

"What if the entry is not in the woods?"

"What do you mean?" Jerry came closer.

"The one place kids are never allowed to play, except on Halloween, is where?"

The Suntychs answered at the same time. "The maze."

Melissa silently clapped her hands in excitement. "Mr. Ferguson always monitored it well on Halloween, he said so no one would get lost for long. Maybe it was so no one would discover the secret entrance."

"And the rest of the year his Dobermans roamed it to discourage any curious town folk." Wanda snapped her fingers. "So, what if Carl shot that guy coming out of the woods, not going in."

"Wait. Wasn't he shot in the back?"

"That's right, Jerry. But he could have seen Carl and turned to run into the woods for protection."

"True." Jerry bobbed his head.

"That would mean Bubba headed for the cave entrance hidden in the maze. He saw Carl, started to run back into the cover of the woods and Carl stopped him in his tracks."

"Bubba?"

"Exactly. Bubba Huffman was the man that was killed that night. Tommy Reynolds, the guy who was killed in the park, used to live on the dairy farm and work odd jobs on the grounds as a teenager. He hung out with Bubba and Adam Archer's stepbrothers, one of which is Carl."

Jerry nodded. "I remember Tommy Reynolds. A troublemaker. He was quite a few grades above me. Still, he had a reputation. Scrub Oak's own James Dean."

"I've heard that."

Melissa touched her shoulder. "Wait. You think Carl killed him, too?"

"It's possible, I guess, though I hate to admit it. Bubba Huffman and Tommy Reynolds led his brother, Colton astray back in the day. My guess is they were part of the gang that robbed the jewelry store in Burleson."

"Well, it makes sense." Jerry shrugged.

Wanda felt the adrenaline returning. "And if Tommy discovered the entry to the bootlegger cave while he worked on the grounds as a teen, it would also make sense he and this gang would head there to lay low. Let's go."

They power-walked from the edge of the woods to West Elm and headed up 8th Street. By the time they got to the lane, Wanda's calves burned but she kept on going. The gate remained open, but this time two patrol cars were parked at the edge. Good. Todd and Adam must have convinced Chief Brooks and Jim Bob to walk up the lane as well.

They crossed the lawn crouching low to the ground, stopping momentarily to crouch behind statuaries, bushes, and the gazebo. At last, the three got to the beginning of the maze.

"Do either of you recall how to get to the center?" Wanda glanced at the couple.

"I think I do." Jerry started inside. "I have always had a good sense of direction."

"Great. I'll follow you two then."

A few minutes in, Wanda realized she did not have any sense of direction at all. The moon shone high above now, casting shadows along the hedge branches, like eerie short hands ready to grab and snare her. She kept her eyes to the ground directly in front of her to avoid the creepiness from getting to her.

Suddenly, she no longer followed the Suntychs. When had she lost them? Tagging along in the rear in silence, they probably hadn't realized she dropped out of sight.

Oh, dear. Where was she? The hedges held no clue. She spun around and peered down a path that seemed identical to the one she walked. Should she venture ahead or try to retrace her steps?

Who did she kid? She had no clue as to where she had come so far. She whispered their names. "Jerry? Melissa? Where are you?"

Only the swoosh of the hedge leaves in the summer night breeze responded. Swallowing down her anxious thoughts, she kept going, remembering her task. Look for anything that might be an entrance to a hidden cave.

As she bent to peer into a small break in the hedges, a squawk and fluttering of feathers halted her with a gasp. A bevy of quail scurried across her path, probably just as frightened as she felt.

She wobbled to a concrete bench and slumped onto it, pressing her hand to her double-time thumping heart. Calm down, calm down.

The little girl fear of losing her parents in the

amusement park begin to surface. She fought it back. They had found her then. Someone would find her now.

She sniffled and hid her head in her hands. Inside her mind, the little girl version of herself cried out for mommy and daddy. Then a quiet voice reminded her she had a Daddy—one who was wiser, all knowing, and more powerful than any father on earth.

Sucking in a deep breath, she called on Him for help.

CHAPTER TWENTY-EIGHT

Voices. Men's voices. They were whispered, but she heard them plainly. And the voices grew louder.

Wanda realized they were in the maze with her. Were they coming in or going out? Police or burglars? She didn't know. But she better hide.

She crawled under the bench and wiggled her back half into the hedges. From her new viewpoint all she could she was the ground in front of her, but in the moonlight, maybe most of her body would remain hidden. Thank goodness she had worn dark colors.

The voices became more distinct and she heard footsteps.

"I tell you the cops are inside the mansion. We can't go back that way."

Carl's voice. She recognized it.

"That doesn't mean they know about the secret door into the cave." The second man's voice sounded more gruff, harsh. Could it be the notorious Butch McClain? Wanda's heart skipped, half in fear, half in excitement.

The steps came closer and she saw two pairs of shoes. One had boots on, the other scuffed running shoes with grungy, frayed shoestrings. Both wore jeans, crusted at the bottom with dirt. The odor of male sweat reached her nose. She pinched it with her fingers.

The feet stopped. One pair turned to face the other pair. "I don't like this. I know I saw two people in the woods. They're looking for us, man. You shouldn't have gone to that woman's house."

The second voice, Carl's, raised a bit, almost into a snake's hiss. "Look. You don't tell me what to do, okay? We needed food, and she owes me so I knew she'd oblige. Remember, that old lady schoolteacher noticed you in the grocer's. We don't want that happening again."

"Yeah, yeah. Okay." The sneakered feet kicked some of the ground.

Ah ha, it was Butch. She closed her eyes for a minute to calm her nerves. Then she heard him speak again.

"So, what do we do? Go back to the cave?"

"Yeah. Odds are they won't find us. If they start coming from the house, we can make a quick exit and head to Aurora's basement. I have a key."

"Right."

The feet turned away.

Wanda scooted out from under the bench. As she did something hard pressed against her hip. Her phone. She'd forgotten she had it in her pocket. Of all things.

She quickly texted Todd and the captains. *Cave*

entrance in maze. Have spotted Butch and Carl. Hurry.

She decided to follow them, her ears on high alert as she lagged behind enough to remain out of sight but still barely hear their footfall. At least, the night breeze had subsided so the hedge leaves no longer rustled. Thank you for that, God.

Then she remembered Melissa and Jerry. She had to find them before they came upon the thieves. Jerry had a weapon, and she was confident in his expertise in using it, but she didn't want them to be in danger. Not on her watch.

As she rounded a corner, she saw the men stop and peer back. Wanda plastered herself against the hedges to stay in the shortening shadows and held her breath

"You hear something?" She recognized Butch's gruff growl.

"Nah. You?"

"Guess not. Probably one of those stupid quails again."

She waited until she heard the footfall resume then followed a bit further down the path and saw them turn right.

When she got to the edge, a hand grabbed her mouth. She struggled to scream but a male voice whispered in her ear.

"Shh. It's me, Jerry."

He released his hand and she gulped in air.

"You scared the bejeebers out of me. Where is Melissa?"

He motioned with his head down another path. Finger

to his lips he beckoned her to follow him.

Wanda hesitated. She wanted to catch up to Carl and Butch, find the cave entrance, and . . . what? Helpless and unarmed, what could she do? Nothing but put herself in harm's way.

Resigned, she nodded and followed him. He found Melissa and the three wound their way to the entrance of the maze in time to meet Todd and Adam.

Wanda rushed to them. "They are in the maze, headed back into the cave."

Jerry came up behind her. "I know the way now. Come on."

Todd and Adam nodded and the three headed back in.

Melissa let out a small whimper.

Wanda grabbed her hand. "All we can do is wait and pray."

They sat on the grass, cool and slightly damp from the dew. Melissa tapped her fingers onto her knees and kept taking deep breaths. "I thought by retiring and moving back here where he grew up, I would no longer have to worry about him." She let off a nervous laugh.

"It'll be okay." But Wanda's gut twisted as well. *Lord, don't let anything happen to Todd, either.*

Several more men came dashing across the grounds. Ray O'Malley arrived first. "The Chief and Jim Bob are in the tunnel coming from the house. They've got them trapped."

"How do you know?"

He pulled out a small listening device. "Figured out the radio channel they use to communicate. Don't tell them, though." He winked.

Everyone else grinned.

Shouts rang out. And then gun fire.

Bam, bam, bam.

One of the shots ricocheted off a statue, sending a puff of marble dust into the night air.

Melissa let out a small whelp.

Wanda jumped to her feet.

Minutes passed. Nothing. Silence.

Wanda closed her eyes to pray. She felt Melissa's cold hand grasp hers. Slowly one by one the others moved into the huddle and bowed their heads in silence as well. Off in the distance, a lonesome whippoorwill cooed its mournful cry.

Julie B Cosgrove

Chapter Twenty-Nine

Footsteps thudded out of the maze. Everyone turned with their mouths open.

Jerry stood at the entrance, his eyes wide with excitement, his chest heaving as if out of breath.

"They got them. It's over."

"Is Todd okay?" Wanda heard her voice wobble. Unshed tears stung her eyes.

"Yes, but Adam was hit in the arm. Nothing serious, I'm sure."

"And Carl?"

Jerry shook his head. "I don't know. He went down. So did the other guy."

Sirens blared into the night air. Their warning grew closer as they bounced into the lane leading to the mansion. The local fire truck, two EMS vehicles, and another squad car dashed over the curb and onto the grass. Red lights whipped off the building, casting an eerie glow in the moonlight.

The county sheriff's cruiser arrived as well. They all

stopped in a half circle about fifty yards from the maze. The EMT's jumped out and pulled gurneys from the vehicles. Firemen ran alongside, carrying red cases of life-saving equipment.

Todd emerged, walking slowly with his head toward the ground. He raised his gaze, nodded to Wanda, and then headed to speak with the other officials. After what seemed like an hour, but probably was only a minute or two, the county men and EMTs pushed into the entrance in the hedges.

Wanda bit her lip. She waited as Todd took his sweet time wandering over to her. Her anxiousness melted as he drew closer. He appeared worn out, the burden of the past week draped over his shoulders. A rookie cop, he had seen way too much violence in a short time. It had to weigh on his nerves.

Her heart opened and she went to him, wrapping him in a hug.

One of the sheriff's men appeared with a large thermos and cups. Todd gratefully took some water and guzzled it down, then wiped his mouth.

Chief Brooks and Jim Bob emerged and swaggered over to greet him. They grabbed some cups of water as well.

Chief Brooks pointed to the house. "Better get forensics over to the mansion. There is a skeleton hidden in one of the panels of the wine cellar. We found it trying to locate the cave entrance. It's obviously been there a while."

Wanda and the others gasped.

"Who is it?" Evelyn's voice came up from behind. Then Wanda caught a whiff of Betty Sue's lavender scent and felt her warm arms wrap her shoulders. She grasped her best friend's hand and leaned against her.

"Don't know, Evelyn." Jim Bob pushed his cowboy hat back from his forehead and wiped his brow. "Think it is a man, though. Maybe a teenager."

Murmurs filtered through the crowd. Who on earth could it be? And how long had it been there?

Wanda swiveled to Betty Sue and Evelyn. They all spoke out the same thought.

"Panel" had been one of the Scrabble words.

Todd stared in unbelief. "Well, I'll be."

Julie B Cosgrove

CHAPTER THIRTY

The crowd grew silent as the gurneys exited the maze. Two were carrying zipped bags. One carried Adam, half propped with one arm bandaged and an IV drip in the other.

Wanda trotted over to him. "Are you all right?"

He grabbed her hand and smiled. "I will be. The bullet may have shattered the bone. I think they are taking me to surgery."

Wanda gazed up at the attendant who nodded.

"Then I will be there when you come out of recovery. Promise. Do you want me to call your wife?"

He sighed. "She will be fit to be tied, but yes. If you don't, the hospital will. I'd rather she hear it from a friend."

"Of course." She followed alongside the gurney until it got to the EMS van. Then she waved as it drove away.

Todd drew her to him. "He's a tough old bird. He'll be fine."

She nodded with a sigh. "I know. I feel responsible, though."

"Me, too. I should have shielded him better."

She swung around. "No. Then you'd be in there." She pointed to the emergency vehicle headed back to the lane.

"Sorry, I didn't believe you about those Scrabble words." He began to walk her to her car. Evelyn and Betty Sue followed as the police began to cordon off the maze and the mansion as a crime scene.

"It's all right, Todd. Half the time I didn't believe it either."

They both chuckled and strolled away with the rest of the dispersing crowd.

Wanda waited until Adam's wife arrived at the hospital a few hours later, her cheeks tear-stained. They hugged.

"He is out of surgery and in recovery. They will take him to a room soon. The doc said everything is fine. They removed the bullet and put in some screws in his humerus bone." She pointed to her left upper arm.

"Bullet?" Mrs. Archer trembled. "What exactly happened, Wanda?"

Wanda hesitated, wondering how much to say and if Adam's wife would blame her for getting him involved in all of this.

About that time, Chief Brooks wandered over and greeted them. He sat down on the other side and explained the whole thing. "Adam became a hero tonight. He assisted us in a manhunt, knowing we are short-staffed in this town to handle such a thing. He was doing what he could to protect the citizens of this community and I plan to suggest to the mayor that Adam receive a medal of honor."

As Mrs. Archer dabbed her eyes, the Chief raised his gaze to meet Wanda's questioning face and then returned his attention to Mrs. Archer.

Wanda's dignity became bruised. Did she not matter to him? Maybe his pride wouldn't let him admit she had helped. He had made it clear he was not in favor of a neighborhood watch, or her *meddling*, as he called it.

That tiny voice in her soul asked if perhaps he was protecting her by not bringing her into the whole thing. She sighed, convicted. She needed to start thinking better of people and not get her feelings battered.

As the Chief rose to leave, he reached out and took her hand then whispered into her ear. "I will recommend one for you, as well. Wanda. You've earned it. Thanks."

Wanda sat back in astonishment. Wonders never ceased.

Wanda returned to her house as the pre-sunrise's pink glow came over the horizon to shoo away the dark. Never had she recalled being so weary. A frantic Sophie greeted her, bouncing and whining. Wanda patted her, gave her some milk bones, and waddled off to have a long, hot shower.

She barely recalled folding back the covers before she slumped onto the bed and fell asleep.

About noon, she awoke. Her muscles ached and her stomach growled. Sophie sat next to her, inches from her face, her head cocked and soft brown eyes searching.

"Okay. Okay. I am fine. Let's go get you breakfast before you dig up my flowers again."

As Sophie slurped and slopped up her food, Wanda fixed herself a huge breakfast of scrambled cheesy eggs, sausage, and French toast.

As if he could smell it, Todd knocked on her back door. "Aw, good. You're up."

He edged inside and eyed her plate.

"Come in. Have you eaten? There's plenty."

"Not in a while. Thanks." He grabbed a plate and spooned some eggs and sausage onto it. Then he sat across from her. She divided her French toast and gave him half.

For a moment, the only sounds he made were happy grunts as he shoveled in the hot breakfast. Then he sat back, wiped his mouth, and sighed. "Guess you deserve to be filled in since you were instrumental in capturing those thieves."

She set her fork down. "Oh?"

He rose, grabbed the coffee carafe, and topped off her mug before pouring one for himself. Then he took his time swirling in some cream and sugar.

Wanda bit the inside of her lip trying to remain calm.

A smirk eased over his face. He was playing with her.

"Todd."

He leaned back in the chair and stretched his legs under the table. "One of the bodies was identified as Butch McClain. They found the jewels, well most of them, in the cave hidden behind some rocks. It seems Aurora had pawned a few trinkets in Fort Worth to buy them supplies."

"So, she and Carl were involved. I knew it. Do you think he bumped off Robert so he could have her?"

Todd gazed at her and said nothing.

"Well, the bullets matched, remember?"

He played with the half-folded napkin. "Yep. That they did. Same rifle. But she isn't talking. She has lawyered up."

"And Carl?"

"Dead."

Wanda looked to her plate. "Oh, I see. I figured as much when I saw the body bags coming out of the maze."

Todd scooted his chair closer to the table and learned forward. "Here's the kicker. The guy on the gurney was Colton, not Carl. Carl's remains were behind the panel."

"What?" Her heart stopped beating for a nanosecond. She grabbed her chest.

"Remember when Carl came back and everyone marveled how much he had changed in college? More confident. And a bit more devious in his business dealings. A bit boisterous, too. Though he never broke the law he kinda bent it to build his little car empire."

"Yes, so?"

"It was Colton all along."

Wanda's hand flew to cover her gaped mouth.

"That's right. As near as we can figure it, Colton killed Carl, stuffed his body in a gunny sack filled with lye and shoved it behind a panel in the wine cellar. Coroner believes his remains have been there going on twenty years or more."

"So that means he was killed right out of high school?"

"More like out of college, which would have been about 2002. Doubt if Colton had the smarts enough to pull off the great grades that Carl apparently earned. Though several years apart, the two resembled each other a good deal."

"I remember that."

"Colton had been involved in petty crimes in three states since he ran away from military school. Jailed twice on minor charges. Never incarcerated more than two years or so. The rest of the times the detectives couldn't get any charges to stick. But he could only remain in the shadows for so long. He knew the police would nail him eventually."

"As they did Butch McClain in 2002. The year you suspect Carl was killed."

"Right. We figure he saw a chance to turn over a new leaf and took it. He returned to Scrub Oak as the good brother and made a life for himself."

The French toast in her stomach jumped into her esophagus. And to think Colton had fooled everyone for two decades. "I guess Butch contacted him when he was released?"

Todd got up and put their plates in the sink. As he rinsed them off and put them in the dishwasher, he finished telling her the rest. "Don't know for sure. We figure that Tommy and Bubba had gotten in with Butch. They were positively identified as the three burglars on the closed-circuit television video tape. My guess is that Tommy told them about the cave and how it would make a good hideout. Then one of them must have recognized Colton in town."

"So, he killed them, in the name of ridding Scrub Oak of wanted criminals when in fact he only wanted to keep his identity a secret."

Todd closed the dishwasher and leaned his backside against it. "Possibly. Somehow, he got involved with Butch, though. Maybe he was all along and bumped off his old buddies so he could have a bigger share. We'll never know for sure."

She shook her head in disbelief. "All this time, it's been Colton living here? Unbelievable."

"I know. Sounds like a TV mystery plot, right?"

"And Aurora didn't figure this out? Or Adam?"

Todd shrugged. "Adam didn't. But there had been so much hurt in that situation, I don't think they were ever close."

"No, they never saw eye to eye. Adam Arthur is too by-the-book. Carl liked to shade the black to dark gray."

"Good description, Aunt Wanda. They tried to avoid each other in public as much as possible. I know that much."

Todd returned to his chair.

"Still, Adam felt an obligation to him. He told me as much last night."

"Hmmm." Todd took a sip of coffee. "As for Aurora? Maybe she did figure it out. She always had a thing for Colton from what I understand. She played up to Carl to get Colton to notice her in school. Then he was expelled. Who knows?"

Wanda tried to sort through all this information her nephew had tossed at her. "Too many loose ends."

"I know. Trust me, the State investigators are all over it now. They are looking into Robert's shooting and petitioning the county courts to change his death from accidental to suspicious. Eventually they will unravel it all."

"I hope so."

Wanda got up and went in search for her notebook. She sat back down as Todd poured himself the last of the coffee.

"What is that?"

"The Scrabble words. Maybe they can help."

He laughed. "Couldn't hurt. Though I haven't told the chief about these yet. I like my job."

She rolled her eyes. "Okay, so we know *jewels*, *woods*, *escape*, and *perp* all fit."

Todd edged closer to read her handwriting. "As do *bushes* and *cave*. There was a circle of small bushes in the center of the maze surrounding a statue of the original Ferguson patriarch. If you shoved the statue's base to the side, it revealed the entrance to the cave underneath."

"Wow. So, the entry point was *under* the statue. That word now fits. We know *panel* matches and so does *Candy*. That was Aurora's nickname in high school. Evidently she had a huge sweet tooth."

"I see. Interesting. And *lying* fits because that is what Colton did all along."

Wanda slapped her forehead. "And all this time I took it as lying, as in a body position."

"Easy mistake. What about the words *zero*, *auto*, and *reduce*?"

Wanda rubbed her temples. "I have no idea. We thought *auto* referred to Otto Ford who had bought the dairy farm and built the resort. His nickname was Auto like a car. Did you know he sold the resort to Robert Stewart a few years ago?"

"Really? That is an interesting piece of information. I will pass it along. But perhaps *auto* referred to the business Carl, ergo Colton, went into."

Wanda felt a wave of stupidity splash over her. "Of course. But what about the word *zero*?"

Todd scrunched his mouth to one side. "This may be a long shot, but as we neared the mansion, I noticed that the zero in the address, 101, had come dislodged. It was at an angle." His eyes widened. "By golly. It pointed to the maze."

"Seriously? Todd this is beyond weird."

They stared at her page. Only one word remained—*reduce*.

"Could it mean that Carl's body was reduced to remains?"

"Aunt Wanda, that is a long shot, don't you think?"

She agreed. "I can't figure how it relates to anything. Unless it is Betty Sue always nagging at me to eat healthy and lose some weight."

Todd rose and kissed her on the cheek. "Maybe we will figure it out in the end. In the meantime, I think we should switch to a word game like hangman. It might be safer. We played that a lot when I was little."

She hugged him around the neck and laughed.

Chapter Thirty-One

The next Saturday at nine in the morning, everyone gathered at the courthouse steps. Red, white, and blue buntings flapped in the breeze. United States and Texas flags waved in the hands of the crowd. Under an arch of red, white, and blue balloons stood a podium on a small stage at the top of the stairs that lead into the building. The mayor and Chief Brooks sat on one side, with Wanda and Adam Archer, still in a sling, on the other.

After a short speech, which was a blessing from God because the temperature already hovered at ninety degrees, the mayor presented them each with a medal of honor.

The townsfolk cheered as the high school band struck up a chorus of "For He's a Jolly Good Fellow," led by retired principal Fred Ballinger on trombone. Wanda didn't mind the male reference. She knew it was for both her and Adam.

On the front row stood Hazel, Betty Sue, Evelyn, and Todd. They rose to lead the standing ovation. One by one, her neighbors stood as well. The Suntychs, Frank, Beverly, the Kings, Sally and her sister Priscilla, Barbara the librarian, Zelda and Vlad, and Fix-It Finn. All of the neighborhood watch volunteers were there. On the back row she eyed Mr. Baker clapping and smiling. Aurora was nowhere in sight, but Wanda hardly expected her to attend. The brunch had obviously been cancelled.

As she gazed out on the happy faces, Wanda's heart swelled so big she feared it would burst.

Ben Bolton gave both her and Fire Chief Archer gift certificates for five free dinners at Big B BBQ. Then they each got a coupon for a hundred-dollars' worth of groceries from the Grocery Mart, a bouquet of red roses from Kay's Flowers, and Wanda received a year's worth of free hair stylings from A Cut Above.

Tom Jacobs snapped photos of them for the front page of the *Gazette*. Pastor Thomas then followed with a prayer of praise and thanksgiving.

Finally, the mayor presented Wanda with six signs to be placed around town as soon as the poles were erected, designating the town as a neighborhood watch community.

Someone cried out "Speech."

The mayor stepped back and handed her the microphone.

Wanda cleared her throat. "I do not know what to say. Which is a rarity."

Laughter waved through the crowd.

"I have no words to express my gratitude. Your honoring me today has reduced me to tears."

Suddenly her hand went to her mouth. She gazed at Todd, who glanced at Betty Sue and Evelyn. They all roared with laughter.

"Sorry." She waved her hand. "Inside joke. Seriously though, I am speechless. All I can say is thank you for supporting me. I know our town is in safe hands with our wonderful police department and fire department guarding it. It is my privilege, along with my fellow neighborhood watch volunteers, to support them in any way we can so we can *reduce* crime in our town."

Todd rolled his eyes but grinned. Betty Sue laughed, and Evelyn gave her the thumbs up sign.

The crowd erupted in louder cheers and Chief Brooks, of all people, led them in a "hip-hip-hooray."

Wanda gulped back tears of gratitude as she pressed her hands to her heart.

The meddling little old widow was a respected member of her community at last.

Recipes

Honey Mustard Deviled Eggs

Ingredients:

1 dozen eggs, boiled, halved and yolks removed to a bowl
1 celery stalk finely chopped
Real bacon crumbles (2-3 crisply cooked strips)
3 heaping tbsp mayonnaise - I use Blue Plate
1 ½ tbsp honey mustard dip
2 tsp dried chives
Salt and pepper to taste

Directions:

Mix the yolks and other ingredients in a bowl. Stuff the egg white "boats" with the mixture then sprinkle with paprika. Arrange on a serving dish garnished with parsley or cilantro.

Makes 24

Tarragon Chicken Salad for 6

Ingredients:

2 boiled, boned full chicken breasts (or 4 halves) finely chopped or pulled. I prefer pulled.
1 tbsp fresh tarragon (or cilantro) finely chopped
3 tbsp mayonnaise – Blue Plate is best
4 oz whipped cream cheese spread, room temperature

12-16 seedless grapes (green or red) halved

½ - ¾ c finely chopped pecans or walnuts

½ tsp salt

¼ tsp ground white pepper

Directions:

With a whisk or hand blender, mix the mayo, tarragon, salt, pepper, and cream cheese in a bowl until a smoothe mixture. Fold in the rest of the ingredients using a spatula or flat spoon. Chill for two-three hours. Just before serving, arrange leaves of Batavia or Green Leaf lettuce and scoop a generous portion onto each lettuce "boat." Garnish each scoop with a sprinkle of paprika and a sprig of parsley.

Cheesy Eggs

Ingredients per person:

2 eggs

1 tbsp softened room temperature cream cheese spread.

¼ cup shredded cheese blend (ex: Monterey jack and cheddar)

Dried chives.

Salt and pepper to taste.

Directions:

With a whisk or bullet blender, blend together the eggs and cream cheese. The cream cheese may not blend all the way. That is all right.

Turn the burner onto medium high.

Pour into a skillet and place on the burner.

Begin to blend with a wooden spatula or spoon. Keep folding the cooking egg into the raw portion until all is evenly cooked.

Remove from heat and sprinkle in the shredded cheese and chives, folding them into the fluffy eggs.

Let it stand for a minute for the cheese to melt in, then serve with breakfast meats, along with toast, muffins, or biscuits.

High Tea Cucumber Sandwiches

Ingredients:

One 5-6 inch fresh cucumber

Six-eight slices of bread

Mayonnaise (I use Blue Plate or Dukes)

Salt to taste

Directions:

Skin a large cucumber. I use a carrot scraper.

Thinly slice it into "disks".

Remove the crust from the bread slices.

Lather both sides of the bread with mayonnaise until moist, but don't drench the bread.

Layer the cucumber slices on a piece of bread and cover with another piece.

Slice diagonally or in three "strips".

Easy Crisp Bacon

f you like baked bacon but hate setting off the smoke alarm or cleaning up the mess in the oven, try using the microwave.

Place 3-4 strips of bacon on two layers of paper towel squares.

Cover with two more layers.

Microwave on High one minute plus one more minute per slice.

No need to flip them over.

Let them sit for a minute, then peel them from the paper towels with a fork or tongs.

Toss away the paper towels once cooled.

Bacon will be crisp, evenly cooked, and not very greasy at all.

You can buy ribbed bacon pans for the microwave. Much better than the kind you hang and let drip while cooking - they tend to smoke.

Mouth-Watering Brownies

Ingredients:

¾ c Wesson oil

2 cups sifted flour

1 tsp of salt

4 tbsp of cocoa

1 tsp of cream of tartar

Julie B Cosgrove

½ tsp of cinnamon

4 whole large eggs

2 tsp of vanilla

½ tsp of almond extract

1 ½ cups of finely chopped pecan pieces

Directions:

Preheat oven to 325 degrees.

Combine the dry ingredients until well blended.

Add eggs and extracts, then whip with a fork until smooth.

Fold in pecan pieces.

Pour into a greased and flour-dusted 9x6 glass baking pan.

Bake for 45 minutes or until a toothpick comes out almost clean.

Cool, then slice into squares.

Yields 9-12 depending on slice size

Acknowledgements

I would like to thank Marji Laine of Write Integrity Press for contracting me to write this series, and also Teri Caldwell who carefully edited it for any typos, overused words, and discrepancies.

I would also like to thank the members of the Cozy Mystery Facebook groups such as Crazy for Cozies and Cozy Mystery Village, especially Michelle Wicker, for their support and suggestions. Y'all are a great group of writers and readers. It is fun to hang out with you.

I have included, as a thank you, several real people's names in this book. You now know who you are. I hope you accept my small gesture of gratitude by honoring y'all as loyal friends, readers, and supporters of my mysteries.

To Mike and Wanda Agee and the DJ's at The Journey, 88.3 FM Christian Radio—broadcasting out of Keene, Texas and streaming live—thanks for the background music as I write. The uplifting music, uninterrupted by commercials, helps to keep my mind pure and focused on writing about godly characters.

Finally, I praise my Lord who has given me this talent and desire to write about active, fun, and vibrant seniors. We are never too old to be used for His glory. Life is a mystery, but His love certainly is not. It is faithful and everlasting.

May you always know, no matter what happens in this imperfect world, God is there, and He cares.

Julie B Cosgrove

About the Author

Julie B Cosgrove has been making up stories almost as long as she has been walking. Not falsehoods, heaven forbid. But tales, plots, and plays, often starring her stuffed animals and dolls.

Growing up with an attorney for a father who also loved nature, Julie learned to observe things many never see like a spider web under a leaf or a sparrow peeking through the lush leaves of a live oak tree. She also developed early on how to methodically gather evidence in order to plead her case.

Her mother loved wordplay games and soon Julie, under her tutelage, became enthralled with the jumbles, crossword puzzles, and find-the-words in the daily newspaper. They had many a battle of wits over games of Scrabble. Julie still has the board and tiles from the set she grew up playing.

At the age of ten, Julie was introduced to the suspense romance novels by the late British author Mary Stewart, who captivated Julie with her vivid descriptions and excellent wordsmithing. When not reading or solving word puzzles, Julie curled up on the floor of the living room to absorb the old Sherlock Holmes (starring Basil Rathbone), Charlie Chan, and Agatha Christie movies offered by the local TV station.

At thirteen, she came to know the mercy and grace of God through His Son, Jesus, and desired to help others discover it in their lives. Her stories took on a deeper purpose, some winning recognition in high school and college.

Then life, work, and motherhood took center stage. But stories still floated in her mind and she continued to dive into whodunnits for entertainment and to play word games with friends offline and online.

As the nest emptied, Julie began writing devotionals for several publications and for the past ten years, her blog, wheredidyoufindgodtoday.com, has touched readers in over fifty countries. She became a writer and editor for CRU as well as an inspirational speaker. Storytelling remained her passion, though.

After publishing seven suspense and romance novels, her sister challenged Julie to write what she loved most to read and watch . . . cozy mysteries, but to write them with a message. Julie queried her publisher who gave her a shot at it.

She was awarded contracts for two cozy mystery series, published between 2015 and 2020. Then Julie had another idea. Combine her two loves of mystery and word games into a series.

Her seventh published cozy, which is the first novel in her third series, The Wordplay Mysteries, is in your hand. Julie hopes you've enjoyed reading how the mystery unfolded in the fictitious town of Scrub Oak, Texas and will return to find out how Wanda, Betty Sue, and Evelyn continue to use the clues through wordplay to solve crimes in future books.

Also by Julie

Three best friends delve into the past, simply building family trees. But sometimes simple things can lead to trouble, and the roots of these trees have deep and perilous connections. Secret ones that don't want to be unearthed.

Find all of the Relatively Seeking Mysteries at Amazon.

Suspense and Mystery from Pursued Books

Thank you
for reading our books!

Look for other books
published by

P

Pursued Books
an imprint of

W

Write Integrity Press
www.WriteIntegrity.com